D0045909

FIC AUC

Auch, Mary Jane.
Out of

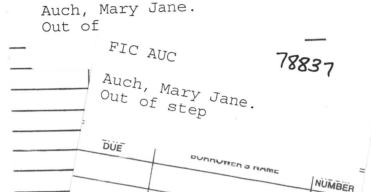

FIC AUC

Auch, Mary Jane.
Out of step

78837

DUE	BORROWER'S NAME	NUMBER

78837

Siskiyou County
Office of Education Library
609 South Gold Street
Yreka, CA 96097

OUT OF STEP

OUT OF STEP

Mary Jane Auch

Holiday House / **New York**

Library of Congress Cataloging-in-Publication Data
Auch, Mary Jane.
Out of step / Mary Jane Auch.
p.   cm.
Summary: After his father remarries, twelve-year-old Jeremy
begins to feel that there is no place for him in a family which
now includes a stepsister his age who is a superb athlete.
ISBN 0–8234–0985–6
[1. Stepfamilies—Fiction.   2. Fathers and sons—Fiction.]
I. Title.
PZ7.A898Ou   1992   92–4704   CIP   AC
[Fic]—dc20

OUT OF STEP

Chapter One

I clung to the boat's rail as we lunged over wave after wave. The spray hit me full in the face, blinding me. Then it cleared for a second. I could see the rocks and the thundering Falls dead ahead. I gripped the rail tighter, throwing my full weight to starboard. The boat shuddered, then began a slight turn. Was it enough, or would we hit the rocks? Even worse, would we be smashed to bits by the Falls?

I grabbed a new handhold and leaned into the fury of the churning water, willing the boat to change course.

"What's the matter, Jeremy? Afraid you'll get washed overboard if you let go?"

I whirled around and looked into the grinning face of Allison, my new stepsister.

"Try this," she said, raising her arms over her head. "Look, Ma, no hands."

"Look, Ma, no brains," I mumbled. I made sure I

said it softly enough so my words were drowned by the roar of the water.

Dad stood with his arm around Kay, his new wife, while my little brother, Timmy, held Kay's hand.

"So what do you think?" Dad shouted. "Bet you didn't have anything like Niagara Falls in Boston, did you, Allison? Right now, you're looking at thousands of gallons of water."

"Well, Dad," Allison said, smiling. "We had the Atlantic Ocean. There's a lot of water in that, too."

Dad laughed, throwing his free arm around Allison's shoulders. "That's a good one, Allison." He looked at me. "Isn't this great, Jeremy? We're a whole new family, and you get a sister just your age. I'm glad we decided to bring everybody along on our honeymoon." The four of them stood there, dressed alike in the blue slickers the crew gave us when we boarded *The Maid of the Mist*. They looked like a family of detergent bottles posing for a vacation picture.

Timmy clung to Kay as if he were afraid he'd lose her the way we lost Mom three years ago. Timmy said he missed Mom, but he was too little when she died to remember her. He just wanted to have a mother again—*anybody's* mother.

I was nine when Mom died, and I could still picture everything about her. Allison might be able to call my father "Dad" after meeting him just a few times, but Kay wasn't "Mom" to me. She was pretty, and friendly enough, and I liked her. But she was still just Kay, not Mom.

Timmy ran over and tugged at my sleeve. "Let's pretend we're on a pirate ship, Jeremy. This will be better than pretending at home, 'cause there's water here and everything."

"Okay," I said, hoping Allison hadn't heard. I hadn't figured Allison out yet, but she didn't seem like the pretending type. When I turned around to face the rail, the magic was gone. *The Maid of the Mist* had made a full turn, and we were pulling away from the base of Horseshoe Falls, heading back down the river to the boat dock.

Timmy looked up into my face, squinting in the rolling mist that still drifted over us. "Please pretend, Jeremy. You can be the captain this time."

"You pretend, Timmy," I said. "I'm tired."

Timmy's lower lip trembled. "Please? You're better at it than I am. I can't think of the right pirate words."

"Ahoy, mate," I said quietly, so Allison wouldn't hear. "Prepare to board the vessel dead ahead. They carry a cargo of gold and diamonds."

"Aye, aye, captain," Timmy shouted. "I'll turn out the lights so they don't see us coming."

"You mean 'douse the lanterns,' " I whispered.

Timmy grinned. "That's what I meant. I'll douse the lanterns."

Most of the other tourists had moved to the stern

to catch a last glimpse of the Falls. Timmy ran
around the bow, putting out imaginary lanterns.
"There, done," he said, breathlessly. "Look at them.
The sailor on watch doesn't suspect a thing." He
pointed to a teenager half asleep on the landing
dock. The kid held the thick rope, ready to throw it
on board when we got close enough. The old magic
started working. Suddenly that guy wasn't just a kid.
He was a pirate.

"Aye, matey," I said. "When we pull up aside them,
ye take the man on watch. The captain is mine."

Timmy's eyes sparkled. "Right-o. I'll slit his throat
with me trusty sword." As he whooshed his empty
hand through the air, I saw the gleam of a blade.
Timmy was getting better at pretending every day.
He was almost as good as Rex, the imaginary friend
I had when I was little.

"Strangling might be better," I said. "Ye wouldn't
want to spill blood on the gold and diamonds."

Timmy squinted at the observation tower above
the landing dock. "Wait a minute, Jeremy. Doesn't
that look like a castle tower? Maybe we should be
knights in shining armor rescuing a princess. See the
mist coming from the American Falls? That could be
the smoke from a fire-breathing dragon."

"You can't change your mind right in the middle
of an adventure," I said. "Besides, the only way to
get to the top of the tower is by elevator. Knights
don't use elevators to rescue princesses."

Timmy looked up at me, water dripping from his

chin. "They could if they wanted to. You said you can do anything you want in your imagination."

"Just make up your mind," I said. "Are we pirates or knights in shining armor?"

I heard someone laugh, and looked up. Allison was standing there, shaking her head.

"I thought you went back to the stern with Dad and Kay," I said.

"I did, but they started playing smoochy-face." She wrinkled her nose. "Then I come up here and find you two playing fairy tales."

"We are not," Timmy said, whipping out the sword. "We're pirates."

"And I'm from outer space." Allison leaned on the rail and looked over at me. "So, what is there to do this summer in your town?"

"Lots of stuff," I said.

"Like what?"

"Well, my best friend, Tony Cibula, and I are putting together insect collections. You can get extra credit for stuff like that in seventh-grade science."

Allison's eyes widened. "You're kidding, right?"

"No, honest. Tony's older brother did projects on insects, leaves and wildflowers and he ended up with A's in the first three marking periods."

Allison slipped off her hood. Her hair had reddish tints in it just like Kay's. Her eyes were big and brown, and you noticed them right away. She looked right at you when she talked, so you almost felt she could read your mind. "Let me get this straight," she said. "Your idea of fun is collecting bugs, right? Don't you play any sports?"

"Sure I do. I'm in the summer soccer league."

Allison gave me a punch in the arm. "Now you're talking. What position do you play?"

"Uh—in the middle," I mumbled. I didn't want to admit that the position I played ninety-nine percent of the time was on the bench.

Allison nodded. "Midfielder? Me, too. I'm a half-back. I like that position because you can really move around to where the action is. Our team was in first place this summer after just three games. So how can I join your team?"

I shrugged. "You have to sign up with the recreation department. It's probably too late."

Allison folded her arms. "When they see me play, they'll let me in, no matter how late it is."

"You're pretty sure of yourself, aren't you?" I said.

"About soccer?" A slow smile spread across Allison's face. "Definitely!"

Timmy pulled on my arm. "Hurry up, Jeremy. It's time to get the gold and diamonds."

"Not now, Timmy," I said.

Allison grinned at me. "Don't let me spoil your fun." She turned back to lean on the rail.

The Maid of the Mist had circled back to the starting position at the dock and the crew was putting the gangplanks in place. Dad and Kay were ready to get off, motioning for us to follow them.

Timmy hung on to his slicker when one of the

crew members tried to collect it. "Try to steal my suit of armor, will you? Take this!" He whipped out a sword again, but this time I couldn't see it.

"Give the guy the coat," I said.

Timmy looked up at me. "But the princess!"

Allison was right behind me, listening to everything and laughing. I yanked off my slicker and handed it to the guy, pushing ahead of Timmy. "There is no stupid princess."

"Come on, everybody," Dad called. "We'll take the tram and show Kay and Allison what the Falls look like from the top." He came back to us with tickets just as an open-sided tram pulled up at the stop.

I climbed into the backseat. Timmy got into the same seat, but he slid as far to the opposite side as he could. "You'll see more over here," I said. "The Falls are on this side."

Timmy turned away from me. "I'm mad at you, Jeremy."

"Come on, don't be that way, Timmy. We're on vacation. This is supposed to be fun."

Kay and Dad waved at us and got into the seat behind the driver. Allison jumped into the seat in front of us just as we lurched into motion. She turned around and looked at Timmy. "You like scary rides?"

"This ride isn't scary," Timmy said.

Allison grinned. "Not yet, but wait 'til we go over the Falls."

"We're just going on a sidewalk," Timmy said. "We've been here before."

Allison shifted sideways in her seat so she could watch Timmy's face. "That's how it used to be, but it was real dull, so nobody would ride on it. Now they've fixed it like a roller coaster. It drops you right over the Falls—about a hundred thousand feet. Didn't you see it when we were on the boat?"

Timmy shook his head, his eyes wide.

"Don't listen to her," I said. "She's never even been here before."

Allison put her finger to her lips. "Shhh! Listen. The guy's telling about it now."

". . . and was killed instantly when he hit the rocks at the bottom of the American Falls," the driver said over the loudspeaker. "The entire body was never recovered, although fragments were found as far away as Niagara-on-the-Lake."

"Whoa! Splat!" Allison said, pretending to drop something over the back of the seat. "Some ride, huh?"

I could see Timmy's lower lip start to tremble. I slid over to his side of the seat. "The guy on the loudspeaker is just telling about people who tried to go over the Falls in a barrel. Remember? The driver we had last time gave the same speech."

Just then, the tram turned off the main path and dipped down toward the American Falls. Timmy's face went white. "Allison was right!" he screamed. "We're going over the Falls!" He tried to dive over the edge of the car, but I hauled him back by his shirt, then wrapped my arms around his middle. "Let me go!" he screamed, kicking my shins with his heels.

Allison patted Timmy's arm. "Relax, Timmy. I was only kidding. This is as far as the tram goes, see? You have to walk down those steps over there to get to the Falls."

Dad and Kay came running over as soon as the tram stopped. "What happened?"

Allison shrugged. "I guess he's scared of the Falls."

Kay picked Timmy up, and he sobbed into her shoulder. "He's probably tired," she said.

I wanted to tell Dad about Allison, but I figured it would only start an argument. I'd have to make sure she didn't try to scare Timmy again, though. Allison seemed to feel she could just take over and do anything she wanted to. I could tell Timmy's life and mine would never be the same again.

We walked down to the little platform that perched between Bridal Veil Falls and the American Falls. The roar of the water made my chest vibrate. Timmy hung on to Dad and Kay with an iron grip. He had finally stopped crying, but every now and then he'd give a little shivery sob.

"It looks as if Timmy's had it for the day," Dad said. "Let's stay on the next tram until we get back to the parking lot. It's almost a two-hour drive to get home."

"Can't we get off for a few minutes at Three Sisters Islands, Dad?" I asked. "That's back away from the Falls. Timmy shouldn't be scared there—unless somebody tells him some wild stories." I glared at

Allison, but she just smiled and tried to look innocent.

By the time we got to the Three Sisters, Timmy was feeling better, but he still hung on to Dad and Kay. Allison rushed ahead, and I followed her across the small bridges between the islands and caught up to her at the farthest point.

There we were, in the middle of the Niagara River, not far from the brink of the Falls. There were no guardrails, and Allison was way out on this flat rock. If I nudged her just one little bit, she would be part of Niagara Falls history—one more statistic for the loudspeaker on the tram.

As I moved closer, I could imagine Allison being caught up in the current, screaming her stupid lungs out. Nobody would hear her over the roar of the water before she dropped over the edge.

"Jeremy?" It was Timmy, slipping his hand into mine. "Allison thinks our pretending game is stupid. Do you think so, too?"

"No," I said. "Who cares what Allison thinks, anyway?"

"Well, remember back at the boat? I knew there wasn't really a princess or a dragon or pirates. But you always said if you could imagine something, it was just as good as being real."

"Yeah, it is," I said, staring at the churning water. In my mind I could see Allison's head bobbing in the rapids. "It certainly is!"

Chapter Two

The house seemed weird with Kay and Allison in it. It was more than just having two extra people around, like when I had a couple of friends sleep over. Everything had changed. The house didn't belong to me anymore. Even our dog, Rass, had noticed it. He used to sleep most of the day, but now he jumped up every time somebody walked through the room.

Kay had sold all of their furniture, except for an antique rolltop desk that had belonged to her grandfather. Now it sat in the corner of our living room. I took hold of the knob and rolled the wood-slatted cover open. There was Kay's computer inside.

Kay knew a lot about computers. That's how she met Dad—at a computer convention in Boston. Then they wrote letters to each other and talked on the phone for almost a year before Timmy and I met Kay and Allison. Last summer we rented cottages

next to each other for a week on Cape Cod. The first
time I saw Dad looking at Kay, I knew we were
about to get a new stepmother.

"That seems kind of funny, doesn't it," Kay said,
waking me out of my daydream.

"What?" I asked.

"The modern computer in a desk that's over a
hundred years old. It's a strange combination."

"Oh, yeah, I guess." I still felt uncomfortable
around Kay. Except for that week on the Cape and
the wedding in Boston this past week, we hadn't
talked to each other. Now, hearing her voice, I felt
a sudden stab of missing Mom. I turned away in case
I was about to do something dumb like cry.

"I know you used to have a room of your own,
Jeremy. It doesn't seem fair that Allison gets her
own room now and you have to share with Timmy.
I'm sorry."

I wanted to say Allison needed a whole room for
her collection of stupid sports trophies, but I didn't.
"It's okay. Timmy and I get along fine." And Allison
and I don't, I thought.

A shaft of morning light came through the window, making Kay's hair honey-colored, like Mom's.
She even looked a little bit like Mom when she
smiled. She was smiling now. "I've noticed you're
very good with Timmy. Some older brothers aren't
so kind. Mine was a real pill—teased me constantly."

I suppose I should have asked Kay more about her

brother. I could tell she was trying to be friends, but I didn't want to get to know her. There was still part of this house that belonged to Mom. Sometimes it felt as if she were still alive. I could pretend she was off getting groceries or walking the dog in the woods. If Kay stayed a stranger, then she couldn't take Mom's place. "I gotta go somewhere," I said, and bolted out of the house.

I wanted to grab my bike and escape, but Dad and Allison were playing basketball in the driveway. The rusty old hoop hung from the garage by a couple of loose nails, but Allison managed to sink a basket without even jiggling it. Dad's face was red and sweaty. He looked happier than I'd seen him look for a long time.

Every time I'd ever tried to shoot a basket, I missed. Dad tried to be patient with me, but I could see how much he enjoyed playing with a kid who was athletic.

"Nice one, Allison," Dad yelled. Then he spotted me. "Come join us, Jeremy. I'll take on the two of you."

I ducked in the garage and grabbed my bike. "No thanks. I gotta check with Tony about something."

Dad pulled off his T-shirt and wiped his face with it. "I'm beat, Allison. You should go along with your brother and get to know the kids around here."

"Sure," Allison said. "You have an extra bike I can use?"

"The green one in the back of the garage should be okay," Dad said. "Just check the tires. It hasn't been ridden in a while."

I couldn't believe it. Dad was letting Allison have Mom's bike. I glared at Dad, but he was too busy helping Allison get ready to notice. He dusted off the seat and pumped air into the rear tire. "There. That ought to get you where you're going."

"Thanks, Dad," Allison said. "See you later. Maybe we can finish up that game after dinner."

"Boston is playing New York tonight," Dad said. "You want to watch that, don't you?"

"Are you kidding? Who would want to miss a Red Sox game?"

I would, I thought, but I didn't say anything. Ever since Mom died, I usually sat through games on TV with Dad, just to keep him company. I didn't understand half of the rules in either baseball or football, but I tried to act interested. I had the feeling Mom had always watched games just to please Dad, too.

Allison sounded as if she really loved baseball. She and Dad were still going on about some baseball player when I took off. I knew Dad would kill me for leaving without Allison, but I had to lose her before I got to Tony's house. I might have to share my dad with Allison, but I didn't have to share my best friend with her.

I shifted gears and cranked hard down the road. It

wasn't long before I heard some heavy breathing behind me. "So you want to race?" Allison said. "You're on!"

She stood up on the pedals and moved out so fast, I could have been riding a tricycle. Did she have to be good at everything that was even the slightest bit athletic? I was pushing hard, trying to catch up, when I realized Allison was about to pass Willets Road. That's where I turned off to go to Tony's.

"Go for it, Allison," I yelled as I rounded the corner. "There's a big trophy waiting for you at the end of the road."

Before I reached the end of Willets, I heard the breathing again, a little heavier than before. "What's with you?" Allison puffed. "You trying to lose me or something?"

"I yelled to you," I said, not really lying. "I thought you heard me." That part was a lie.

"Well, I didn't hear you. I was about ten miles down the road when I looked over my shoulder, and you weren't there."

"Ten miles?" I pedaled harder. "That's some trick. The road dead-ends in Lake Ontario about a mile from the turnoff."

"Think you're smart, huh?" Allison forged ahead at top speed, while I turned the corner at Kenyon and headed for Tony's house. "See you later," I yelled.

Unfortunately, Allison had wised up. She caught

up to me at Tony's driveway. "I supposed you yelled to me again?"

I tried not to smile as I balanced my bike against Cibulas' barn. "Sure did."

I followed the sound of a motor and found Tony out back on the riding mower. He grinned and turned it off. "Am I glad to see you. Maybe now Dad will let me take a break." He looked at Allison. "Is this your new sister?"

"Stepsister," Allison and I said in unison. It was the first time we'd agreed on anything.

"Yeah, right." Tony took off his baseball cap and wiped his arm across his forehead. He studied Allison for a minute. "So you've just moved here from Boston. What do you think of Ontario, New York?"

Allison shrugged. "I haven't seen much of it yet."

Tony laughed. "There isn't a whole lot to see. Come on in the house. I'm dying of thirst, and I'll show you my latest finds for the project."

We followed him, and waited while he took an inventory of what was inside the refrigerator. He pulled out a large pitcher. "My sisters had some friends over this morning and they drank up all the pop. All we have is this herbal iced tea my mom makes. Want some?"

"I'll pass," Allison said.

Tony poured glasses for himself and me. I could hear some kids talking upstairs. Tony had three brothers and two sisters, so there were always kids around the Cibulas' house.

Tony led the way to the sun porch. Our bug collection was in labeled plastic bags on the card table. "Look what I found this morning. According to my bug book, this thing isn't even supposed to be in this area."

Allison turned a chair backward and straddled it. "Guess your bug never read the book." She looked around, drumming her nails on the table. "So let me get this straight. You guys go around killing bugs and looking them up in books?"

"We don't have to kill them," Tony said. "I turn off the pool filter at night and skim the bugs off the water every morning."

Allison's face lit up. "Pool? You have a pool around here somewhere?"

"Yeah," I said. "It's out behind the barn."

Allison jumped up. "All right! Lead me to it!" She burst through the screen door and hopped across the backyard, yanking off her sneakers, then jumped into the water with her clothes on. But instead of fooling around like a regular kid, Allison started doing laps, which is hard to do in a round, aboveground pool. She only got in about three strokes each time before she had to turn and go back.

Tony and I stood by the edge of the pool for a few minutes waiting for her to slow down, but Allison kept on churning like a machine. Finally we gave up and went back to the screened-in sun porch.

"Does Allison ever just relax?" Tony asked.

"Maybe when she sleeps," I said.

"You two certainly don't seem like a brother and sister."

"We're not, we're . . ."

"I know," Tony interrupted. "I just meant I can't picture the two of you living in the same house."

I sat down and took a sip of my iced tea. It was so bitter, it made me shiver. "I can't picture us even being friends. We don't like any of the same things. She loves every sport that was ever invented, and I'm a total klutz. But Dad wants me to make her feel at home."

"Get your Dad to sign her up for the summer soccer league in Casey Park. That'll get her out of your hair."

"Then I'll have to see her more than ever."

"Sure," Tony said, "but the chances of you being on the same team are slim. If she's so nuts about sports, she'll probably be practicing all the time."

After about half an hour, Allison came across the yard, dripping wet. She found her sneakers where she had dropped them and jammed her feet into them.

"You want a towel?" Tony called to her.

Allison shook her head. "That's okay. The wind will dry my clothes and hair on the way home. Thanks for the swim, though. It was great."

"Any time," Tony said. I kicked him under the table. Tony flinched, but he didn't say anything.

Allison waved as she took off down the driveway. "I'll take you up on that."

By the time I got home, Dad was busy fixing dinner. He'd had to learn how to cook when Mom died, and he found out he really enjoyed it. He didn't cook regular stuff, though. He made fancy gourmet meals, and some of them were pretty weird. He looked up when I came into the kitchen. "Oh, good, Jeremy, you're home. Run out to the garden and get me some vegetables, will you? I need beans, eggplant and tomatoes."

"Sure, Dad."

I took Rass with me. I had to watch him, because he loved to eat tomatoes. Last year he wiped out Dad's whole supply. As I bent over a row of beans, I heard Allison's voice. "Yuck! Those beans are purple."

"They turn green when you cook them," I said. "Nothing in this garden is the usual color. We have blue potatoes and corn, white eggplant and yellow tomatoes. Dad thought the weird colors would make Timmy and me want to eat vegetables."

"Did it work?"

I shook my head. "Not really. The garden makes Dad happy, though. He's always looking through seed catalogs for some strange new vegetable."

"What's this?" Allison pointed to a pink pumpkin growing inside a plastic mold.

"This is the first year he's tried that," I said. "As the pumpkin grows, it fills in the mold. When you take off the mold in the fall, the skin is supposed to be in the shape of a face."

"Then you could paint it for Halloween," Allison said.

"I guess so." This was the first time Allison seemed interested in anything but sports.

Out of the corner of my eye, I saw Rass trot by with a tomato in his mouth. By the time I'd wrestled it away from him and fastened him to his cable run, Allison had gone into the house.

All I had to do was mention the soccer league at the dinner table, and Dad got all revved up about it.

"Thanks for reminding me, Jeremy. Bob Fisher is the head of the town recreation department and I know him from Rotary. I'm sure he'll let Allison sign up late."

Kay cut up Timmy's pork chop for him. "Are you playing soccer this summer, too, Jeremy?"

I nodded.

"I'm glad the two of you will be doing something together," Kay said.

"We won't be together," I answered, realizing I had almost shouted it. "I mean . . . there are already too many kids on the Hornets."

"Allison," Dad said. "You're not eating your egg-plant. I made a special sauce with the golden toma-toes and some garlic."

Allison poked at her food. "I hate vegetables. I hardly ever eat them, except for mashed potatoes, and then it has to be the powdered kind."

Dad speared a bean with his fork and waved it to make his point. "An athlete needs to practice good nutrition. There's nothing better for you than fresh-picked vegetables just barely steamed until they're tender."

"It's my fault that Allison doesn't like vegetables," Kay said. "I always used canned or frozen vegetables to save time, and then I boiled the daylights out of them. Try these, honey. They're wonderful."

Allison forced a forkful of eggplant into her mouth. She chewed it for a long time, then made a face when she swallowed it. Dad looked annoyed. So—finally there was something that Dad and perfect little Allison disagreed about. If I knew Allison, though, she'd be eating veggies by the bushel any day now, just to butter up Dad.

Allison and I helped Kay clear the table while Dad made the phone call about getting Allison into soccer. "It's all set," Dad said a few minutes later. "Bob says there's room for another player on the Hornets. I think I swayed him by saying that Allison will be the Hornets' star player."

"Great," I said. "The Hornets could use a star."

Dad caught the sarcasm in my voice and followed me into the kitchen. "I'm sorry, Jeremy. I just wanted to make Allison sound like a great player so I could get her on your team. Otherwise you might have games scheduled at the same time on different fields, and I'd be running back and forth to see you both."

"It's okay," I said, scraping plates into the garbage. But it wasn't okay at all.

Allison appeared in the kitchen doorway. "When's the first practice, Dad?"

"Tomorrow at two o'clock," Dad said, "and a game at six. Speaking of games, the Red Sox will be on any minute."

Dad and Allison disappeared into the living room, leaving me to finish clearing. When I went back to the table, I noticed that Allison had carried exactly one plate and one fork into the kitchen.

"Hey, Jer, will you read to me now?" Timmy asked.

"Sure. Just help me clear the dishes."

I'd been reading to Timmy every night since Mom died. It used to be the only way he could get to sleep, and I'd just keep going until his eyes closed and his breathing got slow and regular. Now it was a habit, and Dad took us to the library every week for our supply of new books. Timmy liked the way I could read with different voices for the characters. That's how we got started on our pretending games. Now Timmy could do voices as well as I could.

I showed Kay the best way to load the dishwasher, then called to Timmy. He ran ahead up the stairs, but I stopped by the door to the living room. Dad and Allison were both sitting on the couch, leaning forward with their elbows on their knees. A rim of flickering blue light from the TV outlined their profiles. Like father, like daughter, I thought.

Chapter Three

I didn't have to see Allison much the next day. She slept most of the morning and went to soccer practice in the afternoon. I couldn't face going through practice with her, but I biked over to Casey Park to show her where it was. Then I told the coach I had a dentist's appointment, so I had an excuse to leave.

Allison jumped right into the warm-up and started dribbling the ball around the field, passing it back and forth with some other kids. Why did Dad have to get her on my team? There were seven other teams in the league, for pete's sake.

At dinner that afternoon, all anybody talked about was Allison's first game. Dad kept asking her questions about practice.

Then he turned to me. "How about you, Jeremy?"

"How about what?" I mumbled through a mouthful of mashed potatoes.

"Practice," Dad said. "How did it go for you?"

"I had to get my teeth cleaned, Dad. Did you forget?"

"I guess I did forget. You never asked me for money to pay the bill."

"They said they'd send it," I said, avoiding his eyes. My face felt hot. Now I was lying to my own father, and it was all Allison's fault.

"We'll drive you kids to the park," Dad said.

"Tony and I are riding our bikes over. I'm supposed to pick him up." Tony wasn't on the team, but he came to my games anyway, for moral support. He couldn't play sports any better than I could.

Dad shook his head. "All right, but you're not riding your bike home from the park if it's getting dark."

"It's summer, Dad. It gets dark late now."

"The coach said we have to get there early," Allison said.

Kay started gathering up the serving dishes. "We can all go early. There must be lots of things to do in the town park. We can hang around until the game."

While the rest of the family got ready, I took off down the road, glad to get away. When I got to Tony's house, he was waiting for me in his driveway, so I didn't have to stop. He pushed off and rode next to me. "Is Allison coming to your game?"

"Worse," I said. "She's on my team."

Tony shook his head. "What were the odds of that happening?"

"The odds were real good with my father pulling strings."

"Maybe it won't be so bad," Tony said. "At least it will give you two something to talk about."

"You know what my games are like, Tony. I spend more time on the bench than on the field. If Allison is as good as she says she is, she'll make me look like an idiot."

"Maybe Allison exaggerates," Tony said. "How good was she in practice?"

"I didn't go. I told the coach I had a dentist's appointment."

Tony nodded and let the subject drop. As we rode along in silence, I pictured how the game would be—Allison scoring goals, and me sitting on the bench. When we pulled into Casey Park, she was already on the field, practicing. Dad watched from the sidelines, smiling proudly. He looked up briefly and waved as Tony and I dropped our bikes by the bench.

Tony pulled a bunch of small plastic bags out of his pocket. "I'm going to check out the bug population by the lake. There should be some different varieties here."

"Have fun," I said. I wished for Tony's sake I could get more excited about bugs. Truth was, I didn't like bugs much better than sports. What was the matter with me, anyway? Everybody but me had a burning interest in something.

"Don't look so depressed," Tony said. "I'll be back in time to see you play."

"You'll be in time even if you catch the last ten minutes of the game," I said. That was all the coach ever let me play, and then only if we were way ahead and could afford to lose points.

A lot of the soccer players were being dropped off in the parking lot. Most of the parents left and came back later for the game. Not Dad. He was right by the field, watching Allison's every move. I could see Timmy on the playground with Kay, laughing.

I didn't feel like getting on the field for warm-ups. There was nothing much going on anyway, because the coach hadn't arrived yet. I walked to the drinking fountain to kill time.

"Jeremy! I was hoping I'd run into you here." It was Mr. Hollis, my English teacher from last year. I almost didn't recognize him because he was wearing shorts and a T-shirt instead of regular clothes.

"Hi, Mr. Hollis. Do you have a kid playing soccer?"

He smiled and shook his head. "My daughter is a little young for that, but I need to talk to some of my students from this past year about a project. Since Casey Park is where the action is, I figured I'd find most of you here. Those I miss, I can call tonight."

"What's the project?" I asked.

"Writing a play," he said.

"You have the wrong person, Mr. Hollis. I wouldn't know the first thing about writing a play."

Mr. Hollis laughed. "I didn't mean for you to do this single-handedly. It's a group effort. Some of you kids showed real talent for writing last year. You especially, Jeremy. You have a vivid imagination. My plan is to have a summer writing club to develop a play. If it turns out well, we'll put it on for a school assembly this fall."

"Mr. Hollis, I don't think I . . ."

Mr. Hollis held up his hands. "Just give it some thought, Jeremy. I'll schedule the meetings around the soccer games, if that's a problem. The first meeting will be here at the park next Friday at six. You can call me at home if you have any questions. By the way, is Tony Cibula around tonight?"

"He's over by the pond," I said.

"Thanks. He's on my list, too." Mr. Hollis waved and started down the path.

The coach was calling out positions when I got back to the field. My name wasn't called, but Allison was a starter. Big surprise.

All the parents sat in lawn chairs on the sidelines. Dad and Kay were just a couple of people away from the bench. Timmy was sitting in front of them on a blanket.

I could see Mr. Hollis talking to Tony over by the pond. He was the kind of teacher who could make you want to try new things. I never knew I could write until I was in his class.

Tony came running over as soon as he finished talking with Mr. Hollis and slid into his usual spot next to me on the bench. "What do you think about Hollis's writing club? You going to do it?"

"I don't know. It might be fun, writing a play." I traced my name in the dirt with a stick.

Tony poked me with his elbow. "What are you doing, practicing your autograph? 'Jeremy Dillon, famous playwright.'"

"I have a better shot at that than at 'Jeremy Dillon, famous soccer player,'" I said. "Did Mr. Hollis say who else was going to be in the club?"

"The only one he mentioned was you. I guess we'll find out when we go to the first meeting."

"*If* we go," I said. "I haven't decided anything yet." I hadn't been paying any attention to the game. Suddenly the parents along the sidelines started screaming like crazy. Somebody was running the whole length of the field, dribbling the ball.

"Hey," Tony said, yanking on my shirt, "that's Allison. Look at her go!"

The crowd went bananas as Allison popped the ball into the goal. Then all the kids on the team mobbed her, giving her high fives and slapping her on the back.

Dad jumped out of his chair and turned to the father next to him. "That's my daughter, you know."

"I didn't know you had a daughter," the guy said.

"I do now," Dad said. "That's Allison, my new stepdaughter. I think she's going to be the athlete in the family." Dad stood there watching Allison, bursting with pride. I never saw him look like that over anything I did. As he sat back down, Dad glanced at me, but he turned away as if he didn't know who I was. Then he did a sort of double take and grinned. "What do you think of your sister, Jeremy? Some player, isn't she?"

A few of the other parents looked over and smiled, as if they felt sorry for me. Didn't Dad understand how humiliating it was to be sitting on the bench while Allison scored a goal? I looked away and pretended to be watching the game.

It got worse. By the fourth quarter, the score was three–nothing in our favor. Allison had scored all the goals.

The mother next to Kay leaned over to Dad. "This is just thrilling. We lost the first two games this season, and my son was so discouraged. Your daughter has been a bolt of lightning. The whole team is playing better tonight."

"Thanks," Dad said. "We're real proud of Allison."

The coach put me in the game for the last ten minutes, as usual. It seemed like an hour. I never even got near the ball and spent most of the time just standing around like an idiot.

Then, in the last few seconds of play, Allison got the ball again. She passed it to me. I was so shocked, I didn't know what to do with it. Nobody in his right mind ever passed the ball to me.

"Go, Jeremy!" I heard Dad yell from the sidelines. Before I could do anything, a player from the other team slipped the ball away from me. Then Allison went after the ball and got it back. As she charged down the field with it, somebody started chanting and the whole crowd joined in. "*Al*-lie, *Al*-lie, *Al*-lie!" I didn't watch, but I could tell by the uproar that Allison had scored another goal.

The final whistle blew, and the team went nuts. Everybody was congratulating Allison. Dad ran over and hugged her. "Way to go, Allison!"

I was standing there, feeling like a jerk, when I remembered what Mr. Hollis had said. Maybe Allison was good at sports, but I had other talents. I put my hand on Dad's arm to get his attention. "Dad, my English teacher from sixth grade wants me to join a writing club this summer. He says I have real talent. We're going to write a play."

Dad barely glanced at me. "Huh? Oh, great, Jeremy." He turned back to Allison, patting her on the back.

"Come on," I said to Tony. "Let's get out of here. Tony and I are riding our bikes home now, Dad."

"Sure, that's fine, Jeremy." If it had been pitch dark with a raging thunderstorm, I'm sure he still would have let me ride home. One thing was for sure—Dad was a heck of a lot more impressed with soccer players than he was with writers.

Tony and I started out. We could still hear the commotion as we rode away. "You don't need to worry about finding friends for Allison anymore," Tony said. "She seems to be adjusting fairly well."

"Very funny," I mumbled.

We rode in silence for a while. That's when I got thinking. "What's the big deal about soccer, anyway?" I said. "Who couldn't kick a soccer ball down the field and get it into the goal?"

"You," Tony said.

"Thanks. Some friend you are."

"You asked a question and I answered." Tony grinned. "I've known you all your life, remember?"

"But I've never really tried to be good in soccer, Tony. I've just put in my time. Soccer has to be one of the easiest sports to play. Look how big the ball is."

Tony laughed. "What does that have to do with how hard it is to play?"

"Everything! Think about it. In tennis you have to whack a little tennis ball with a racket. That's got to be pretty hard. In baseball, you have to hit this little baseball with a bat—even harder, right? In golf you have to get this really tiny golf ball into a really tiny hole. Now *that's* skill."

Tony pulled into his driveway ahead of me. "So

let me get this straight. If the ball is big, the game is easy, right?"

"Not necessarily. A basketball is big, but the basket is small. But think about a soccer goal. It's huge! You'd have to be blind to miss it. It's like standing in your driveway and kicking the soccer ball into the garage."

Tony eyed me suspiciously. "What are you leading up to?"

"I'm going to start taking soccer seriously," I said. "I'm really going to practice until I get as good as Allison. Even better than Allison."

Tony nodded. "I was afraid that's what you were leading up to."

Chapter Four

Allison's new name was Allie. That's what everybody called her after the crowd chanted her name at the game. It seemed to fit her better, anyway. The name "Allison" sounded to me like it belonged to the kind of girl who would like ballet better than soccer.

I went to practice the next day with a whole new attitude. The coach blew his whistle. "Okay, kids. Let's start out with three laps around the park."

Allie took off so fast, I didn't even see her go. I followed at my usual relaxed pace, but kept dropping back farther and farther in line as kids passed me. So what if I couldn't run as fast as the other kids right now? If I really put some effort into practicing, I'd be outrunning them all before long. I put on a new burst of speed and passed a few of the slower kids.

We'd only gone around the park one and a half

times when I thought I was going to have a heart attack. I wasn't used to running hard. I slipped behind some bushes to catch my breath. Allison was way out in front, and she didn't look winded at all.

Some heavy clouds were starting to roll in, and one of them looked just like a dragon with fire coming out of its mouth. Too bad Timmy wasn't with me. He loved to find pictures in clouds.

When the team came around again, I jumped in behind the last kid and even passed a couple more of them before we reached the coach.

Next we took turns kicking the ball into the goal. As usual, I missed every time. That didn't matter. I could practice kicking a ball into the garage at home.

Then the coach divided us into two teams for a scrimmage. That was one of the few chances I ever got to play. Usually, I just stood around, trying to avoid being where the ball was. This time I even got the ball and dribbled it a few feet before I passed it off to a girl on my team.

"Way to go, Jeremy!" the coach shouted. I couldn't remember him ever praising me for anything before.

The sky was getting really dark now. Heavy black clouds rolled in from the west—the direction of our house. You could hear a low rumble of thunder in the distance. A flash of lightning streaked across the sky. "That storm is closing in," the coach said. "How many of you have to ride your bikes home?"

About half of us raised our hands.

"Okay. You kids take off now," he said. "You should just about make it home before the downpour. The rest of you can practice kicking some goals until your rides come. And remember, we're still playing tonight unless there's thunder and lightning at game time."

Allie and I and a few of the other kids started out on our bikes. As usual, Allie raced ahead of me. That was fine. I didn't feel like talking to her anyway.

As I was heading down our road, the first few drops fell—big ones that splattered on the hot pavement, making steam rise up in little puffs. By the time I reached our house, the downpour was slacking off, but I was drenched. Allie was sitting on the front porch, perfectly dry, drinking a glass of milk.

"What took you so long?" she asked. "I thought you got lost."

I ignored her and went into the house. I was digging around in the refrigerator for a snack when I heard the screen door slam, and Allie came in. "It stopped raining. Want to practice with me?" she asked. "There's plenty of room in the side yard. It's almost the size of half a field."

"You don't think I know how big my side yard is?" I snapped. "Where do you think I've been practicing?"

"No offense," Allie said, dumping her glass in the

sink. She turned and looked at me with those mind-reading eyes. "So, you want to practice or not?"

"Can't," I said. "I'm busy."

I ran up the stairs to my room. I wasn't ready to practice with Allie yet. Maybe later, after I'd had a chance to get better on my own. Then I wouldn't feel so stupid trying to play in front of her. I pressed my face against the screen on my window so I could see around to the side yard. The screen was still damp from the rain, and it had a sharp, metallic smell.

I could just barely see Allie dribbling the ball at first. Then she did some fancy footwork and reversed directions, coming around to the backyard. She turned again, and the ball seemed to wind itself around her feet and go exactly where she wanted it to go. She must have sensed me watching her because she looked up before I had a chance to duck out of sight. "Come on out," she called. "I can show you a few tricks."

"I told you before. I'm busy."

"Jeremy, I didn't know you were back from practice," Kay said, sticking her head into my room. "How did it go?"

"Coach cut it short," I said. "We got rained out."

Kay picked up some of Timmy's stuffed animals from the floor and put them on his bed. "I'm so glad the storm was a short one. I've planned a picnic in the park for before the game."

Kay was really getting into this soccer thing. I suppose she was used to watching a lot of games, being Allie's mother.

As soon as Dad got home from work, we headed for the park. We found a picnic table, and Kay and Timmy unpacked the basket. Kay had made three kinds of sandwiches and had packed bananas and cake for dessert.

I had this sinking feeling in the pit of my stomach, the same feeling I got before every game. I started stuffing myself to try and get rid of it. I always did that. It never worked—in fact it usually made things worse—but I always forgot that until it was too late. Allie just ate bananas. I devoured three sandwiches and about eight cookies.

"Ease up a little, Jeremy," Dad said. "You don't want to be playing on a full stomach."

"Allie's eating," I said.

"The bananas are for energy," Allie said. "I always eat them before games."

I would have eaten a banana, but I was too full. "May I be excused?" I asked.

Dad looked up. "Where are you going?"

"I just want to walk around a little."

"Good idea," Dad said. "Allie and I will join you in a minute. We can all discuss game strategy. You're playing the toughest team in the league tonight."

I struggled up from the bench. My stomach felt

like lead. "That's okay, Dad. I think I need to be alone."

Dad smiled. "Sure, son. Need to get psyched for the game, right?"

"Yeah, that's it," I mumbled.

I went over by the swimming area at one end of the pond and sat on the grass, watching some little kids splashing around in the shallow roped-off part with their mothers.

Tony and I had practically grown up in this park. It always had seemed like a friendly place to me, but tonight I wasn't so sure. Some people are cut out for sports and some people aren't. Deep down, I knew I wasn't, and I hadn't had enough practice to make up for my lack of talent.

Pretty soon it was time for the game to begin. The coach had us do a few warm-up exercises. When we did jumping jacks, I could feel all those sandwiches and cookies colliding in my stomach. I tried not to think about it.

"Okay," the coach said. "Here's the lineup." He read off a list of names and positions. He didn't read my name, but Allie was a starter again. She ran onto the field with the other kids. I went to sit on the bench, but I stopped myself. I couldn't go through another game watching Allie from the bench. And if I didn't speak up, I'd never get out on that field.

"Excuse me, Coach," I said. "I really want to play this game."

He looked surprised. "Okay, Jeremy. I'm glad to see you taking more of an interest in the game. You did pretty well at practice today, so I'll use you the first time we need a sub."

Dad and Kay were setting up their lawn chairs, and Timmy had already settled in on his blanket. Dad was searching the field. When he saw me sitting on the end of the bench, he smiled, but I could see the look of disappointment on his face.

I couldn't keep my mind on the game. The parents were yelling and cheering a lot, because we were winning. Allie racked up two goals in the first quarter.

When I started watching other things that were going on, I saw an orange bike coming into the park. It was Tony. He spotted me and came over. "How's it going?" he asked. "You look like you're still alive."

"That's because I haven't been out on the field yet."

Tony sat on the ground next to the bench. "Is Allie playing pretty well, as usual?"

"Pretty well? She has two goals, and the game's barely started."

"Here comes goal number three," Tony said. We watched as Allie dribbled the ball around two guys and a girl from the other team and sank it into the goal. The crowd went wild. Dad was on his feet, cheering.

"I was stupid to think I could play this game like Allie. I couldn't be that good if I practiced until I was eighteen."

Tony shielded his eyes from the sun so he could watch the action. "You're too hard on yourself. Why don't you ask the coach if he'll put you in?"

"I did ask him. He said he'd put me as a sub later. Now I'm sorry I said anything. I should have kept my mouth shut."

Tony nodded. "You're probably right. Is it my imagination, or is every kid on the other team about a foot taller than you?"

"Thanks, Tony. You really know how to make a guy feel great."

Just then the ref blasted on his whistle.

Noah Predmore, one of the kids on our team, was lying on the ground, and this big red-haired kid with the number twelve on his shirt was getting yelled at by the ref.

"Sub!" the coach shouted. "Jeremy, go in for Noah."

Tony pushed me off the bench. "Go on, Jer. And if anything happens, I want you to know it's been great knowing you. I'll also make sure that the extra credit for the science project gets awarded to you posthumously."

"Thanks," I said. "That makes me feel much better."

Noah came limping off the field. "Watch out for Number Twelve," he said. "He's a killer."

I ran to Noah's position as sweeper and turned to face the other team. A whistle blew, and about half a second later this huge red-haired kid was coming at me with the ball. I couldn't move—couldn't twitch a finger. And there he was getting closer, slow and graceful like a ballet dancer, with his red hair rising up and drifting down with each step. I saw both of his hands reach out, just before he plowed into me. As I went down, he tripped over me and landed on my stomach. I tried to roll over so I could get up, but our legs were all tangled up and I fell back again.

Suddenly I heard this voice saying, "Get off my brother, you big stupid jerk!" There was Timmy on the guy's back, pounding him with his little fists.

It was like this weird dream. Kay came running over—still in slow motion—and tried to pry Timmy loose. Timmy let go suddenly and he and Kay fell over backward, knocking over the ref. It looked like a strike at a bowling alley, only the pins were people.

The ref helped Kay up and she and Dad pulled Timmy off the field. This time the ref not only yelled at Number Twelve, but he pulled out a red card. That meant Number Twelve was out of the game. Did the ref have to wait until I got killed to do that?

I managed to get up on my hands and knees. If there had been a woodchuck hole handy, I would have crawled into it. It was bad enough getting knocked down in my first few seconds of play, but having my six-year-old brother try to rescue me was humiliating. I could hear laughter coming from every direction. Allie was staring at me in disgust. As Dad helped Kay and Timmy off the field, he glanced back over his shoulder at me. He didn't look happy.

"You okay, kid?" the ref asked.

I opened my mouth to answer him. That's when I threw up all over his sneakers.

Chapter Five

I couldn't get off the field fast enough. Kay came running over to me. "Jeremy, are you all right?"

I pushed past her without saying anything.

"Leave him alone," Dad said. "I think he wants to be by himself."

For once, Dad understood me. I ran over to the bushes by the pond and threw up again.

"Hey, Jer?" It was Tony.

"Just leave me . . ."

"Yeah, yeah, I know," Tony said. "I just thought you might want to go home, and you'd need a bike." He set his bike down on the ground next to me. "I'll hitch a ride with our neighbors. Their kid is on the other team."

"Thanks." I doused my face with cold water from the pond. "You're right. I need to get out of here."

Tony nodded. "That's what I figured. Call you tomorrow."

I rode hard all the way home, thinking maybe the pains in my legs would block out the pain inside. I knew one thing. I was never ever getting on any athletic field again. Except for gym, which I couldn't get out of. But at least in gym there were other kids who hated it just as much as I did.

I was a fool to try to play soccer just to please Dad. The other kids on the team were all nuts about the game. Allie spent almost every waking moment dribbling a stupid soccer ball in the side yard. With her around, I'd never be able to impress Dad anyway. Why should I do something I hated just to compete with her? It was useless.

I finally pulled into our driveway. Rass was waiting for me in the kitchen. He stood up and wagged his tail, pulling his lips back into a smile. Poor dog. Nobody paid as much attention to him as Mom had. "Come on, boy," I said. "I think we both could use a walk."

We took off across the back field, over the small wooden bridge and into the woods. Rass was so excited, he kept running ahead. Then he'd come back, wiggling all over from wagging his tail so hard. This was the path we took with Mom in the old days, after supper. She'd always change out of her work clothes into jeans, make herself a cup of coffee, and then call to Rass. I usually went with her, but I hadn't gone down this path since her accident. At first it reminded me too much of her. Then, I don't know why, I just never did it again.

Rass had disappeared. I whistled for him, and he came crashing through the brush. Weeds and new saplings choked out a long section of the path. Then the woods opened up with big old trees, spaced much farther apart. This was where we gathered maple sap when I was little. We never got very much. It took forty gallons of sap to make one gallon of syrup, but we all looked forward to doing it every spring.

I found a rusty metal spout in the trunk of one of the maple trees. The bark had grown up around it, so it wouldn't pull out anymore.

We kept going, Rass leading the way, until we came to Mom's favorite place. She used to call it "the cathedral." An opening in the canopy of leaves overhead made an eerie light in this one spot. There was a fallen log where we used to sit and watch Rass as he sniffed under tree roots, looking for something to chase.

I sat down on the log. The ends had started to rot, and the bark was covered with green velvet moss. Rass sat next to me, whining quietly. "You miss Mom too, don't you, Rass?" He sniffed around the log. Suddenly I heard a clinking sound. Rass had knocked over a coffee mug. Mom must have left it here the last time she came out. It was cracked and filled with leaves and dirt, but I knew it was hers.

I picked it up and turned it over in my hands. Suddenly I was so mad, I couldn't help myself—I threw the mug down, and it split in half on a big rock. "It's all your fault," I shouted. "You left us and now everything's going wrong. You should have been a better driver. Lots of people were out driving in the rain that day. You were the only one who had to skid into a truck and get yourself killed. You should have been more careful. You had a family to take care of. *Me* to take care of! I hate you!"

I threw myself on the ground and sobbed. I couldn't stop for a long time. Rass nuzzled me and tried to lick the tears from my cheek.

"I didn't mean that," I whispered, when I could talk again. "I know you didn't get killed on purpose. It's just that things are such a mess."

I pulled myself onto the log and looked up at the hole in the leaves where the light was coming through. "I don't know if you can see what goes on here from wherever you are, but I'm not doing so hot. Dad has this new wife, Kay. She's really nice. I hope you don't mind about that. But I can't figure out where I fit in anymore. Timmy likes Kay a lot, and you can't blame him. I mean he really doesn't remember you. He was so little.

"And Dad, well, he's got this new stepdaughter who does all the things he always wanted me to do. I can't be a jock, Mom. I have my own stuff I like to do. I wish Dad could see that. I just . . . I just wish . . ." I started to cry again. "I just wish you were still here, Mom. I wish everything was back the way it used to be, because I don't know what to do anymore. I just made the biggest fool of myself that anybody ever made in his life."

Rass pushed his head under my hand to make me pet him. I looked around the woods. There were a few birds flying from tree to tree, heading for their nests. The sun was starting to go down, making golden streaks through the trees. Rass and I had to start back while we could still see the path. I wasn't sure whether Mom had heard me or not, but I felt a little better. I could always come back here again if I needed to talk to somebody. Even if I was only talking to a dog and a bunch of trees, it helped.

I had just reached the path when Rass started acting edgy, as if somebody was in the woods with us. "What is it, boy?"

I could sense it, too—that prickly feeling you get when you know somebody's watching you. Rass's ears perked up, then he started running toward a shadowy figure on the path. It was a woman.

I almost called out, "Mom," then realized it was Kay. I was glad I hadn't made a fool of myself again.

"Jeremy, are you okay? I'm terribly sorry about what happened with Timmy. And then I had to make things worse by getting tangled up with the referee."

"Yeah, we must have put on a pretty funny show," I mumbled.

Kay laughed. "Can you imagine what we looked like? I'm so glad you can see the humor in it, Jeremy. You know, every tragedy has a funny side, only sometimes it takes a while before you can see it."

If I lived to be a hundred, I'd never see the humor in what happened today. Kay might be nice, but she

sure didn't understand kids. Of course with a daughter like Robojock, she hadn't been around a normal
kid.

"You just had a phone call from your teacher, Mr.
Hollis. He said it was about some club. He wants to
change the night, and you're supposed to call him
back."

"Oh, yeah. Writing club," I said.

"Why, that's wonderful! I had no idea you could
write, Jeremy."

Yeah, and I can read and tie my shoelaces, too, I
thought. I hate it when grownups try to act interested in something even when they're not. Kay had
this wide-eyed "I'm fascinated with everything you
say" look on her face. All the way back to the house
she kept asking me stupid questions that I answered
with "yes" or "no."

Dad, Allie and Timmy were at the kitchen table
having ice cream.

Timmy had a chocolate chin. "I got that guy good,
didn't I, Jer?"

Allie snorted. "Yeah, and Jeremy got the ref's Ni-
kes good. The poor guy had to wash them off in the
pond and finish the game barefoot."

"Never mind that now." Dad shoved a dish of ice
cream across the table. "Here, Jeremy. I just dished
this up for you."

"No thanks," I said. "My stomach still doesn't feel
right."

"I could eat seconds," Allie said. "If it's okay."

Dad gave her my dish. "I guess you earned yourself another helping with all the energy you put out tonight."

"The team won," Timmy told me. "Four to one. Allie made all the goals."

"Sounds like Allie won, then," I said. "Not the team."

Dad looked at me. "Don't be upset about what happened, Jeremy. It was just a freak accident. You'll do fine in the next game."

"There isn't going to be a next game," I said, heading for my room.

Dad followed me to the foot of the stairs. "Please don't give up, Jeremy. What happened to you today couldn't happen again in a million years."

Halfway up the stairs, I turned around to face him. I wanted to scream at him for trying to make me into something I wasn't. Then I realized he didn't care what I did. Allie was the kid he'd always wanted. Dad didn't need me anymore at all. There was no point in trying to discuss it with him. "I don't like soccer," I said quietly. "I'm quitting the team."

Dad moved over to let Timmy run up the stairs. "Are you discouraged because your sister is such a good player? Because if that's it, she and I can both help you practice and get better."

"It has nothing to do with Allie," I said.

Dad smiled. "I'm glad to hear you say that, Jeremy. People are good at different things. Allie's a natural athlete. Your abilities lie somewhere else."

Where's that, Dad? I thought, but I didn't ask it out loud.

Just then Allie ran into the living room and turned on the TV. "Come on, Dad, we're missing the Pan Am games."

Dad reached out toward me with his hand, but I turned away and climbed the rest of the stairs. When I got to the top and glanced over the railing, Dad was gone. I could hear his voice and Allie's over the blare of the TV.

Timmy burst out of our room, carrying one of his favorite storybooks. I tried to take the book, but Timmy pulled it back. "Kay said she'd read to me tonight, Jer. You can do it another time, okay?"

"Whatever you say," I said. "It's no big deal."

Even Timmy was pulling away from me. As I walked down the hall, I realized that I'd been reading bedtime stories to Timmy for myself as much as for him. We always curled up in the corner of the couch, and when Timmy leaned his head on my shoulder, I could smell his hair. It surprised me each time it happened, because suddenly we were back in time, with Mom reading to both of us. Smells made me remember more than anything else.

Reading to Timmy did something else for me. It made me feel that somebody needed me. I tried to think of who needed me now, and I couldn't come up with a single name.

Chapter Six

I got up late the next morning. I wolfed down some cereal and was halfway out the door when I remembered to call Mr. Hollis. He wanted to change the meeting, but was afraid it would conflict with my soccer game. He seemed pleased when I told him I wasn't going to play soccer after all.

Allie was practicing in the side yard, but I managed to head out for Tony's house without her seeing me.

Tony was in the pool, skimming up the night's catch. "We got some good stuff today," he said. "Look at this." He carefully lifted a bright red dragonfly from the net and set it on the rim of the pool. "Isn't that a beauty?"

"Yeah, it's nice." I could tell Tony wasn't going to say anything about what had happened at the soccer game. That's the way Tony was. Once something was over, it was over. He wouldn't talk about it unless I brought it up.

"Did Mr. Hollis call you?" I asked.

"Yeah," Tony said. "But I'm not going unless you do. You have a game, don't you?"

I settled down on the deck. "I know my fans are going to be disappointed, but my soccer career is over."

"At least you went out with a big splash." Tony grinned at me. "So does this mean you're going to join Hollis's club?"

"I guess so. We could at least go see what it's like. That wouldn't mean we were signed up for good, or anything."

Tony waded across the pool. "I'm going to turn the rubber raft over. Sometimes bugs collect under there during the night. Take the rest of the good stuff out of the net, will you?"

Dead bugs all looked alike to me, but Tony was an expert. So far he'd been able to identify seventy-nine different kinds of insects. I was trying to pick out the specimens that still had all their parts when I heard him yell, "Geez! Look at this!"

Something dark dove and streaked across the bottom of the pool. "I never saw anything like it," Tony said, reaching toward me, but still keeping his eye on the thing at the bottom of the pool. "Quick, give me the net."

"I didn't get all the stuff out of it yet," I said.

"Never mind. Just give it to me."

Wading slowly so he wouldn't make ripples in the water, Tony stalked the thing. It was bumping up against the side of the pool, as if it was trying to find a way out. Tony made a sudden lunge. "I got it," he said, holding out the dripping net.

The thing struggled fiercely to get loose. It was about three inches long and oval shaped. "Quick, take that glass jar over there and put some water in it. Whatever this is, I think it must live in water."

I did what he said. He turned the net upside down over the jar and the thing fell into it with a plunk. It started swimming frantically into the sides, looking for an opening. We held it up so we could see it magnified through the glass. It was dark brown, and its back looked like bony plates instead of squishy bug stuff. Its two front legs were claws, and the two sets of back legs were flat, like the oars of a boat.

"No wonder it can move through the water so fast," I said. "It looks like a crab."

Tony shook his head. "No, it's a bug. I'm sure of that from the way it's built. But it's the biggest one I ever saw."

The bug had quieted down so we could study it for a few minutes. It looked almost prehistoric—the kind of bug that dinosaurs might have slapped at with their tails.

Tony jiggled the jar to get it moving again. Suddenly the bug came up over the edge of the jar and dropped into the pool with him. Tony jumped back.

"Watch out," I said. "That thing is heading right for you."

Sure enough, instead of being scared of people,

this bug was swimming after Tony as if he were going to be its next meal. Tony thrashed across the pool to the ladder.

"It's still coming. Get out of there," I shouted.

Tony hit the first step of the ladder and jumped the other three. I could have sworn the bug leaped out of the water, going after his heels, as he got out.

I ran over to the deck. We knelt on the edge, staring into the water. The bug was diving and swimming from one side of the pool to the other. "That thing can do laps faster than Allie," I said. "What the heck is it?"

Tony got up. "I don't know, but I'm going to find out." He charged into the house and came back with his bug book.

Tony flipped through the pages. "Sometimes when the pool gets a little green I see things that swim like that. But they're small—about the size of a fingernail."

"Maybe this one has been taking vitamins."

"Here it is!" Tony pointed to a picture that looked exactly like the thing in the pool. "It's a giant water bug."

"Big deal," I said. "I could have told you that."

"No, really. That's it official name." As Tony read, his eyes got wider. "Wow! This says it drinks blood. It can suck the guts out of a frog and leave nothing but a pile of skin. And it can give a vicious bite to a human if you mess with it."

"Yeah, well, I guess you messed with it," I said.

"Now what happens? Is this the end of swimming for the summer?"

"Are you kidding?" Tony grabbed the net. "I'm going to catch that thing."

"And do what with it? Use it as an attack bug to keep people out of your pool?"

"Just be quiet and go get that big jar over there. Fill it about half full of water."

"If you think I'm holding that jar while you drop a bloodsucking bug into it, you're crazy."

"Okay, I'll do it myself." Tony didn't get back into the water, but followed the bug around the edge of the pool until he could snatch it up in the net.

This time the bug seemed to know what was coming, and it was harder to get it into the jar. When Tony pushed it with a stick, the thing grabbed on and wouldn't let go. Tony shook it loose so it couldn't crawl out of the jar. "Man! This is the neatest bug I've seen in my whole life."

"Still playing around with your little bugs?" It was Allie. She'd ridden over on Mom's bike. This time she was wearing a bathing suit, as if she expected us to invite her to go swimming.

I glared at her. "Who asked you to come over here?"

Allie shrugged. "Tony said I could come over anytime, didn't you, Tony?" Allie's eyes widened when she saw the bug. "What is that thing?"

Tony held the jar out to Allie, making her back off

a little. "It's a giant water bug. It can suck the guts right out of a bullfrog."

"Or even a woodchuck," I said. "All it leaves is the skin."

Allie grinned and started to poke at the bug's back. "Yeah, right. Does it bite people?"

"It can take your finger off," Tony said.

Allie pulled back her hand. "Well anyway, what I came over for was a swim. Do you mind?"

"We caught this in the pool," I said. "There's probably others in there."

"You ever think about upping your chlorine level?" Allie asked.

"I like to keep it low so it doesn't bleach out our bugs," Tony said.

Allie walked around the pool a few times, checking out the bottom, before getting into the water. "I don't see any more giant water bugs, so I'm going in." Pretty soon she was doing her usual laps.

"Why didn't you tell Allie to get lost?" I said. "She doesn't have to hang around with us. She's got the whole soccer team to be friends with. She's the big shot of the team, for pete's sake."

A sly smile spread over Tony's face. "Let's see what a big shot Allie really is. Follow me." We went into the house, and Tony started digging through his little brother's toy box. There was still stuff in there from when Tony and I were little. "Here it is." He held a small plastic toy.

"It's your old windup submarine. So what?"

"It's almost the same size as the bug, Jeremy. If we put it in a jar and accidentally spill it into the water, she's going to think it's the real thing."

"We can't, Tony. Dad would have a fit if he heard we tricked her like this."

"But that's just it," Tony said. "She'll feel so stupid for falling for it, she won't tell anybody."

"I still don't think we should do it. After all, she's my sister now."

Tony put his hands on my shoulders. "Look, I've lived with sisters all my life and I've learned one thing. You gotta get them before they get you. Allison's been making you look like an idiot ever since she got here, right?"

"Well, sort of, but . . ."

"Now it's Allison's turn to look stupid." Tony wound up the toy, and we watched as it clicked across the floor.

We found another jar and went back to the pool. I placed the jar on the rim. Allie was still grinding out laps. "Hey, Allie," I yelled. "Want to see the bug again? We're going to let it suck the guts out of a frog."

Allie stopped swimming and stood up. "Yeah, sure. You really think it can do that?"

"You bet it can," Tony said. "And we found a really big, juicy . . . oops!" He tipped the jar into the pool, and at the same time I released the wound-up submarine. "Uh-oh! Watch out, Allie. I just lost the bug!"

The dark shape streaked across the pool. "It's heading for you, Allie," I yelled. "Get out of there, quick."

Allie's face went dead white, even with her tan. "I can't get to the ladder. The thing's got me blocked!"

"Then jump over the side," Tony shouted. "It's really mad, now. Once that thing chomps on to your leg, you'll never be able to get it off."

The toy bounced off the side of the pool, then headed back toward Allie. This was better than we'd imagined. It looked so convincing, I could feel the hairs standing up on the back of my neck. Allie screamed as she scrambled up the side, dropped over the edge and landed with a thud on the ground. She slapped at her legs and feet. "Is it on me? Get it off!"

"It's okay," Tony said, grinning. "You made it."

Allie climbed back up on the deck, her fists clenched. "That thing could have eaten me alive. You dropped it in the pool on purpose."

"It was an accident," I said. Then Tony and I started laughing.

"Oh, yeah? I'll show you an accident." Allie grabbed me by the shoulders and shoved me into the pool. When I surfaced, the submarine was coming across the pool. I reached out and caught it. "What's the matter, Allie? Are you afraid of a little bug?" I threw it, hitting Allie in the foot.

She staggered backward, then looked at the thing on the deck. It was making a ticking noise that got slower and slower, then stopped. "Wait a minute." Allie picked it up. "This is just a toy. It's not what you had before."

"No, it isn't," Tony said, picking up the real bug jar. "We were just playing a little joke on you."

"A joke!" Allie's fists clenched. "I hate both of you." She ran off the deck and picked up Mom's bike, then came back to the edge of the pool. There were tears in her eyes. "You know, when Mom talked about marrying your father, I was really excited about getting two brothers. Timmy turned out to be great, but you know what you are, Jeremy? You're a real loser." She turned and rode down the driveway, her bike tires spitting gravel.

I pulled myself up on the deck. "I guess we shouldn't have done that. It was a pretty mean trick."

"Yeah, but at least it was just a trick," Tony said.

"What do you mean?"

"Think about it," Tony said. "When Allie pushed you into the pool, she thought she was shoving you in with a man-eating bug."

"But she was just getting back at me," I said.

Tony held the jar in front of his face. "You were only playing a trick on her." His eyes and the bug were magnified by the water. "Allie really wanted to hurt you."

Chapter Seven

I didn't see Allie when I got home. That was just as well, because I wouldn't have known what to say to her. Now I knew she liked me even less than I liked her. And she had called me a loser. No matter how disappointed Dad was in me, he'd never called me that.

When I went into the living room, Timmy was holding the ladder while Kay measured a window. "Kay's making new curtains and she says I can help, Jeremy."

"What's wrong with the old ones?" I asked.

Kay stepped down from the ladder. "Nothing. I just thought it would be nice to have something new."

"Mom made the old curtains," I said. "You're not going to throw them out, are you?"

Kay brushed the hair from her eyes. "Of course not, Jeremy. I didn't realize your mother had made these. Why don't I wash them and we'll hang them up again? We could paint the walls, though. Don't you think a lighter color would be nice?"

"Mom painted these walls," I said. "She liked them dark. I do, too." I slammed out of the back door. Pretty soon I heard the screen door slam again, and Timmy came running after me.

"Jeremy, that's not fair. Now Kay's not going to make curtains, and I won't get to help her." Tears streaked his cheeks.

"Good," I said. "Boys aren't supposed to make curtains anyway." I turned and headed toward the woods.

Timmy pulled at my shirt. "That's not what Kay says. Kay says you can do anything you want, and it doesn't matter if you're a boy or a girl. In our 4-H Club, the boys are gonna learn to sew and cook just like the girls, and the girls are gonna build things out of wood and . . ."

"You don't belong to any 4-H Club," I said.

"I do now," Timmy said, proudly. "Kay's starting one. She says I need to have more friends my age."

"Oh, yeah? I don't see her starting up any 4-H Clubs for me so I can have more friends."

"She will if you ask," Timmy said. "I know she will. I'll go ask her." He started running back toward the house.

"Never mind," I yelled. "Come back here."

He came back slowly, wiping his nose with the back of his hand.

I squatted down to his eye level. "We haven't

played pretend in a while. What do you want to be? Pirates?"

Timmy thought for a minute. "I know! Let's play pretend soccer."

"That's the only kind of soccer I know how to play," I said. "But I think we could find something better than that."

Timmy ran over and grabbed the soccer ball that Allie had left in the side yard. He dribbled it toward me, missing every few steps and backtracking to get the ball. "I'm Allie," he said. "You be the crowd."

"I'm one person. How can I be a crowd?"

"You gotta yell '*AL*-lie, *AL*-lie, *AL*-lie!' " He kicked the ball and ran after it, then stopped when he realized I wasn't yelling. "Come on, Jeremy. You're not playing right."

"Let's be something else," I said. "How about astronauts?"

Timmy picked up the ball and clutched it. "No, I don't want to be astronauts. I'm Allie." He kicked the ball into the side yard, shouting "*AL*-lie, *AL*-lie, *AL*-lie!"

Just what I needed. Another Allie in the family.

"Forget it, Timmy." I turned to head for the woods.

"Jeremy?" Kay was following me down the path. "Can I talk to you for a minute?"

"If it's about the curtains and the paint," I said,

"I'm sorry. Go ahead and fix them any way you want. It's your house now."

"No, it's not my house," Kay said. Her voice sounded a little shaky. "It's our house. And if there's something that reminds you of your mother, I don't want to take it away."

"Big deal, curtains," I said. "Besides, I lied about Mom making them. She bought them. You can change anything you want."

"Are you sure? I'm not trying to take your mother's place, you know. I just want to make things as pleasant for the five of us as I can." Kay twisted her gold wedding band around her finger. "That's why I'm not starting a new job for a while. I want us to have a chance to get used to each other first."

I wanted to say I wouldn't get used to Allie in a million years, but I just shrugged.

"Well, that's all I wanted to say. I . . . um . . ." Kay nervously looked at her watch. "We'll be leaving for the game pretty soon. Make sure you're home in time, okay?"

"I'll ride over to the park with you, but I have my meeting tonight."

Kay's face brightened. "Oh, that's right. Your writing club. That sounds exciting, Jeremy. I'm sure you'll come up with something wonderful."

Timmy came running across the yard, yelling "*AL*-lie, *AL*-lie, *AL*-lie!"

As he tried to run past her, Kay grabbed him and

gave him a hug, brushing the hair out of his eyes. Mom used to do that to me all the time. Timmy and I had the same kind of straight slippery hair that slid right back in our eyes as soon as it was combed in place. It had been a long time since anybody had brushed the hair out of my eyes, and I missed it.

Kay carried Timmy into the house. I could hear him giggling all the way in.

I decided there wasn't time for a walk in the woods, so I went to my room. I stretched out on my bed for a while, thinking about our new stepfamily. No matter what I did, I seemed to be out of step with everybody in it.

Pretty soon, Kay called me, and we left for the park. At least because of my meeting I wouldn't have to sit through Allie's game tonight. I didn't have much choice about going with the family, though. If I wanted to eat on Tuesdays and Thursdays, dinner was served on a picnic table in Casey Park. Since Dad wanted the whole family to eat together, it was either go along or starve.

I could hardly wait to get through the meal that night. Things were really strained between Allie and me since the giant water bug incident. The more I thought about what she did to me, the madder I got. Allie and I weren't speaking to each other, but neither Dad nor Kay seemed to notice. Suddenly Allie was the center of Dad's life, and Kay was the center of Timmy's. I might as well have been invisible.

Kay had brought along one of Timmy's new 4-H friends, and the three of them were talking about some pumpkin plants they were growing as if gardening were the most exciting thing in the world. Even with all the weird vegetables Dad grew, Timmy had never shown any interest in the garden before.

"I've heard," Kay said, "if you want really big pumpkins, you have to feed them milk."

Timmy burst into giggles. "Can we give them cookies, too?"

Dad was busy pumping Allie up for the game. "I've seen the blue team," he said. "They were playing on the next field last week, and they looked pretty big."

"That doesn't scare me," Allie said through a mouthful of banana.

Dad smiled. "I didn't think it would, but you might talk to some of the other kids about it, so they don't panic."

I wanted to say that if the guys on the blue team were anything like the kid who demolished me, panicking would be the only sensible thing to do. Then I tuned out as Dad went on giving Allie all kinds of advice.

I watched the park entrance for Tony, and pretty soon I saw his bright orange bike coming around the corner. I excused myself and ran to the parking lot to meet him.

"I wonder who's going to show up tonight?" Tony said. "If Pain-in-the-neck is there, I'm leaving."

Tony was talking about Eileen Stepaniak. The accent in her last name was on the second syllable. It was pronounced "pain," which was a perfect name for her. "She'll probably show up, Tony," I said. "That doesn't mean we let her spoil everything."

Tony hunched over his handlebars. "She always has to run the show. You know that."

"Mr. Hollis will keep things under control," I said. Mr. Hollis was the kind of teacher who could keep the class in line and let you have fun at the same time. He used to read all kinds of books to us, and we had great discussions. He even got me to write my own stories.

Unfortunately, the Pain had learned to write stories, too. And there she was, getting dropped off by her mother.

Tony groaned. "She has Heather Dunlop with her. Heather goes along with everything Eileen does."

"Hi, guys!" Mr. Hollis was just getting out of his car.

"Hi, Mr. Hollis," I said. "Are many kids coming out for the club?"

"Your guess is as good as mine, Jeremy. I talked to

quite a few kids, but this is family vacation time, so some might be going out of town. We'll have to wait and see who shows up."

Mr. Hollis went over to talk to the girls. Tony and I spent a long time at the bike rack, hoping somebody else would show up. There was a line of cars coming into the parking lot, but most of them were there for soccer. There were games starting in both soccer fields, plus a men's softball game in the baseball diamond. The whole park was filled with groups of bright-colored T-shirts. I could see Allie warming up with the red team.

"How come so many kids come out for sports and all we can get for the writing club is Heather and the Pain?" Tony mumbled.

"Hang on," I said. "Somebody will show up."

A blue van pulled up, and Bruno Weisgard and his mother got out. They were heading our way, like a couple of hippos on a forced march.

"Oh, great," Tony said, pulling his baseball cap down over his eyes. "Here comes a real writer. It only takes him three tries to get his name right."

"Hey, at least he won't knuckle under to Eileen. Who knows? Maybe he's an idea man."

"Yeah, sure," Tony said. We followed them over to the picnic shelter.

I had been right about one thing. The Pain wasn't any happier to see Bruno than we were. She moved over on the bench so there wasn't room for him.

Bruno sat at a table away from the girls and hunched over, sulking.

"Hey, Bruno," I said. "I didn't know you liked to write."

Bruno sneered. "I ain't doing this sissy stuff. As soon as Ma leaves, I'm going swimming. And anybody who squeals on me gets a taste of this." He held up a grimy fist.

"No thanks," Tony said. "I'm not hungry."

Mrs. Weisgard was talking Mr. Hollis's ear off. ". . . and I'm convinced that Bernard has a creative streak. It runs in the family. I'm a writer, you know."

"No, I didn't know," Mr. Hollis said.

Mrs. Weisgard straightened the ruffles on her blouse. "Well, of course I haven't actually sent anything to a publisher yet, but I'm working on a novel. Well, of course I haven't actually written any of it down, yet, but it's all up here." She tapped her head, beaming.

"Yes, I'm sure it is," Mr. Hollis said. "Well, if you'll excuse me, I'd better begin the meeting. You can come back for Bernard at seven-thirty."

Tony and I slid onto a bench at a third table. Mr. Hollis checked his watch. "Let's get started. If anyone else comes, we can catch them up." He looked around. "For openers, maybe we could all gather at one table."

We all hunkered down in our places and tried not to look at each other.

"Come on, kids," Mr. Hollis said. "This has to be a team effort if it's going to work."

Heather started to move, but Eileen gave her the elbow, and she stayed put.

"Okay, have it your way." Mr. Hollis sat on a fourth table, with his feet on the bench. "You all know we're going to be writing a play, and I hope you've each given it some thought since I talked to you. Let's get some ideas going here. Heather, what do you think our play should be about?"

Heather shrugged. "I don't know. About kids like us, I guess."

The Pain groaned.

Mr. Hollis nodded. "It's always a good idea to write about what you know."

"But that's boring," I said. "Let's do something with some imagination, like outer space."

The Pain groaned again, louder this time.

"Good thought, Jeremy. Do you have another idea, Eileen?" Mr. Hollis asked.

The Pain stood up as if she were going to give a speech. "I think we ought to write our own fairy tale."

Bruno, Tony and I groaned this time.

Eileen gave us a dirty look. "It's not a dumb idea. They even did a play on Broadway that combined several fairy tales. Aren't I right, Mr. Hollis?"

Mr. Hollis nodded. "*Into the Woods.*"

Bruno jumped up and looked around. "Why? Who's coming after us?"

Eileen sighed and rolled her eyes. "That's the name of the play, beanbrain."

"I knew that," Bruno mumbled, settling back in his place.

Tony and I nudged each other.

Eileen cleared her throat. "Anyway, I think there should be this beautiful princess."

"Three guesses who she thinks should play *that* part," Tony whispered. "Princess Pain-in-the-neck."

". . . and every man in the kingdom wants to marry her," Eileen continued.

"No, it's *bury* her," I said, and Tony snorted right out loud, then fell off the bench, laughing.

Mr. Hollis raised his hand. "Let's give Eileen a chance to finish her story."

"Well, that's the whole thing," Eileen said. "The princess just has to choose who to marry."

Mr. Hollis rubbed his chin. "You really don't have a story here, Eileen. Remember when we discussed conflict in class? You have to give the princess some sort of problem."

Eileen shrugged. "But she's beautiful and popular. She doesn't have any problems."

"Maybe she only thinks she's beautiful and popular," Bruno said. "Maybe she's really a stuck-up jerk and all the men in the kingdom decide they'd rather be killed than marry her."

"Yeah," Tony said. He jumped up on the bench, making sword-fighting gestures. "And after they slash everybody's head off there's only this one guy left, and he's got zits all over his face and he hasn't taken a bath in about ten years . . ."

"And . . . and he drools," Bruno shouted. "He's got this slimy drool all down the front of his shirt, and . . ."

"Stop it!" Eileen was almost in tears. "You're ruining my story."

Mr. Hollis stood up. "I think everybody's getting a little carried away here, but this is the kind of group effort I had hoped to see. Let's just toss some ideas around. Who knows where it will lead us? Does everybody like the idea of some kind of fairy tale?"

"Not with a princess as the main character," I said. "I think it should be a prince and not really a fairy tale. Maybe it should be more like King Arthur, with knights and stuff." Ever since I was little, I'd loved stories about King Arthur and his knights.

"I think it should be about a princess," Eileen argued. "And she's beautiful and popular, and there's no guy with zits and drool."

Mr. Hollis took a vote. The girls wanted a princess, and the boys wanted a prince. Then Mr. Hollis made us have a long discussion about it, so the vote would be fair. Since the boys outnumbered the girls, we still won.

We spent the rest of the time arguing about what the prince looked like, how old he was, what the castle looked like and stuff like that. We decided on Andrew for the prince's name. We still didn't have a problem for him, so we broke up early, and Mr. Hollis said that coming up with a plot was our assignment for the week.

As we went to get our bikes, there was a roar from one of the soccer fields. "Allie's game is still going," Tony said. "Let's see how she's doing tonight."

"I don't care how she's doing. I'm sure that's all I'll hear about when I get home."

Tony pulled his bike out of the rack. "Then you won't have to tell your family what a bomb the writing club turned out to be. I knew the Pain would ruin things."

"Yeah, but Bruno isn't so bad. He's pretty funny when he's not beating people up."

As we rode past the field where Allie's team was playing, the group of parents sitting along the sidelines started screaming like crazy. Somebody in red was running the whole length of the field, dribbling the ball.

"Hey," Tony said. "That's Allie. Look at her go!"

"You look," I said. "I've seen enough of Allie's goals to last me a lifetime."

We rode out of the park with "*AL*-lie, *AL*-lie, *AL*-lie!" ringing in our ears.

Chapter Eight

There was nobody around when I got up on Saturday, but I took my bowl of cereal out onto the front porch so I wouldn't run into Allie when she woke up. As the porch door slammed behind me, a startled rabbit bounded across the yard. Then I realized Allie was sitting on the steps.

"Thanks a bunch," she said, closing the sketchbook she was holding. "There goes my model."

"You were drawing that rabbit?"

Allie stood and pushed past me. "What makes you say that? Maybe I just like to stare at things for hours at a time with a pencil in my hand."

"Can I see it?"

She glared at me for a second, then flipped through the sketchbook to the drawing of the rabbit. The body and legs were just sketched in with a quick line, but she had been working on the face and ears. She had drawn them soft and blurry, as if they were covered with real fur.

I guess I'd been looking at the drawing for too long without saying anything, because she suddenly closed the sketchbook. "It's not finished."

"I didn't know you could draw."

"You don't know anything about me, Jeremy. You never ask." She ran into the house, letting the screen door shut in my face.

I was glad I'd planned to spend the day at Tony's. I knew Allie wouldn't come over there anymore.

Dad was in the garage when I went to get my bike. "Oh, good, you're up, Jeremy. I have to take a load of stuff to the recycling center before it closes. Lug those cartons upstairs for me, will you? They're filled with things that Kay and Allie haven't un-packed yet."

"Then let Allie lug them upstairs," I said. "She's probably stronger than I am, anyway."

Dad laughed and slapped me on the back. "Lighten up, Jeremy. I know having a new sister has put your nose out of joint, but you'll get used to the idea."

"But Dad, Tony's waiting for me. We're going to work on some ideas for the writing club."

Dad heaved a bundle of newspapers into the back of the station wagon. "I'm not asking for your entire day, Jeremy. You can get the whole lot upstairs in a few trips. Certainly your writing can be postponed for that long."

I leaned my bike against the garage and picked up the biggest carton. "What if I'd said I was going to practice soccer with one of the kids from the team?"

Dad looked up. "I thought you weren't playing soccer anymore."

"Never mind," I said. "It was a joke." Dad stood there with a puzzled smile on his face as he held the back door open for me. It wasn't a joke though. It was true. Writing wasn't important enough to skip a chore for, but soccer practice—now that was different. Not only would Dad have let me go, he would have offered to drive me over to practice.

Dad never understood what was important to me, but Mom always had. She had been excited about every stupid play and concert I had ever been in at school. Dad went to them, too, of course. But he always acted like a fireman who hoped to be called on his emergency beeper any second.

By the time I dumped the first load of boxes upstairs and got back to the garage, Dad had gone. This time I piled a small box on top of a big carton to save myself a trip. I was doing fine until I got halfway up the steps. Then I tripped on one of my shoelaces, and everything tumbled to the bottom.

There was nothing in the carton but clothes, so it was easy to stuff them back inside. The small box was filled with pictures, and some of them had slid halfway across the living room. I couldn't help looking at them as I picked them up. There were mostly pictures of Allie when she was about Timmy's age. She looked little and kind of shy—not full of herself and bossy the way she was now.

There was a small yellow envelope labeled "Allison's baby pictures." I sat down on the bottom step and opened it. This time there was a man in the pictures, too, holding a tiny baby. He had the same mind-reading eyes as Allie did. It had to be her father.

I didn't remember seeing him in any of the other pictures, so I started shuffling through the box, looking for him. I'd never heard either Kay or Allie mention Allie's father. I had gone through almost all the photos when I heard one of the stairs creak above me.

It was Allie, standing and gripping the railing with fire in her eyes. "What do you think you're doing?"

"Nothing," I said, feeling my face getting red. "I was taking your stuff upstairs and I dropped it. I was picking it up."

"You weren't picking it up. I've been standing here watching you."

I stuffed the pictures back in the box and put the lid on it. "I was just curious. You've never even mentioned your father. I can't find him in any of the pictures except when you were a baby. What happened to him?"

Allie grabbed the box out of my hand. "Mind your own business." She stormed up the stairs and turned when she got to the top. "Don't ask any more questions about my father, and I won't ask any questions about your dead mother."

"Don't call her that!" I yelled.

Allie glared at me. "Why not? That's what she is, isn't she? At least my father's still alive."

After Allie slammed the door to her room, the house was quiet as a tomb.

I felt so rotten, I didn't want to go to Tony's. I didn't want to be with anybody. I went into my room and closed the door. There was a huge lump in my throat, but I felt too sad to cry, so I just sat at my desk, staring out the window. I didn't know much about Allie at all. One minute she was practically a stranger, and the next minute she was my sister. It wasn't fair. You were supposed to grow up with a family, not have it shoved in your face out of nowhere.

How was I ever supposed to get along with Allie? First she yelled at me for not knowing anything about her. Then when I asked about her father, she blew her stack. I'd never understand her.

Pretty soon I heard a car in the driveway, the slamming of car doors and footsteps on the stairs. Timmy burst into our room and jumped on his bed. That was the one problem with sharing a room with him—I'd lost all my privacy.

"Guess what Mom's going to make for me?" he asked.

I whirled around in my chair. "What did you say?"

"I said, guess what Mom is going to . . ."

"Are you talking about Kay?"

Timmy shrugged. "Sure it's Kay. Who else would it be?"

"Kay is not Mom," I shouted. "I don't ever want to hear you call her that again."

"But Jeremy . . ." Timmy's lower lip began to tremble. "I just want to have a mom like everybody else."

"You had a wonderful mom," I said. I reached in my desk drawer and pulled out the pictures I'd been hiding there. Allie wasn't the only one with secret family pictures. I sat down next to Timmy on his bed and held a picture in front of him. "This is you when you were almost three years old. The lady who's holding you is your mother. Your real mother. She's the one you call 'Mom.' "

"But Jeremy . . ." Timmy started to cry.

Right after the accident, Timmy got really upset every time he saw a picture of Mom. He'd cry and call "Mommy" over and over until he fell asleep from exhaustion. We had to hide all of Mom's pictures. I'd been keeping them in my desk. But now Timmy needed to see what Mom looked like, before he forgot her for good.

"Calm down, Timmy. I'm just trying to show you something." I pulled out my favorite picture of Mom. It was taken by the lake. The wind was blowing her hair, and the sun that was setting behind her made it gleam like gold. "Look at her."

"I don't want to." He squeezed his eyes shut.

"Please, Timmy. Open your eyes and look at her. This is your real mother."

"No she isn't," Timmy said. "I never saw her before. I don't know who she is. Kay is my mother." He twisted away from me, then ran for the door.

Kay was standing there, her face red. Timmy clung to her legs, crying. She knelt down and held him for a minute. Then, when he calmed down a bit, she wiped the tears from his cheeks. "I left a surprise for you on the kitchen table," she whispered. "Want to go see what it is?"

Timmy nodded and ran down the stairs.

"Jeremy," Kay said, getting up. "I think we need to talk."

I went over and sat at my desk with my back to her. "I don't feel like talking."

Kay pulled Timmy's chair across the room and sat next to me. "May I see these?"

"I don't care," I mumbled. I heard her shuffling through the pictures and smelled the faint flower scent of her perfume—almost like Mom's, but different.

"Your mother was very beautiful, Jeremy. You miss her a lot, don't you?"

I felt tears stinging my eyes, but I wasn't about to cry in front of her.

"Look, I overheard you talking to Timmy," she said. "I know it upsets you, but I have to let him call me 'Mom' if he wants to."

"You're not his mom," I said. "You're not mine

either." I shifted in my chair even more so she couldn't see my face.

Kay put her hand lightly on my shoulder. "Timmy was too little to really remember your mother, Jeremy. It's not his fault."

"I just don't want him to forget her," I said. My voice sounded as if I were choking.

"You're right about that, and we'll do everything we can to keep your mother's memory alive for Timmy. But I'm sure your mother wouldn't feel you were being disloyal if you accepted me as your stepmother."

"It doesn't have anything to do with me," I said. "I'm too old to need a mother. I can take care of myself."

I felt Kay's hand lift from my shoulder and I heard the scraping of the chair against the floor as she got up. "All right, Jeremy. But there's nothing wrong with needing a mother, no matter how old you are."

After she left the room, I closed the door and cried for a long time. I needed a mother, all right. But I needed *my* mother, not a substitute.

I'd forgotten all about our play until the afternoon of our next meeting. We had our usual pre-soccer picnic in Casey Park. I watched for Tony, and pretty soon I saw his bright orange bike coming through the gate. I excused myself and ran over to the parking lot to meet him. He was gripping a bunch of wadded-up papers on the handlebars. "Did you write anything for tonight, Jer?"

"No, I forgot. You never mentioned writing anything either."

Tony put his bike in the rack. "I thought it up just before I came over. It's awesome. It takes place under the ocean with these guys who can breathe in the water."

"Tony, we were supposed to be writing about a prince."

"I know. This guy's the prince of the whole ocean. That's a lot better than anything the Pain's going to come up with, speak of the devil."

Eileen and Heather got out of Mrs. Stepaniak's car and avoided looking at us until Mr. Hollis showed up and called us over. "Does anybody know about Bernard?" he asked, looking around.

"If we're lucky, he quit," Eileen said. "Or better yet, maybe he died from a terminal case of stupidity."

Mr. Hollis ignored her remark. "I was hoping we'd see more kids here tonight. I guess we don't have too many budding writers in this town." He settled down at his usual table. "But I'm sure you've all come up with some great ideas. Who wants to start?"

"I do! I do!" Eileen said, waving her hand in his face. "I found a problem for the princess."

"It isn't supposed to be a princess," I said. "We decided on a prince, remember?"

"That's right, Eileen," Mr. Hollis said. "Does anybody have any ideas for the prince?"

"I do," Tony said. "It's called *The Prince of the Ocean and the Bloodsucking Water Warriors.*" He smoothed out his wad of papers and began to read. There were little round men with two sets of legs to swim with. They went around sucking the blood out of their enemies, and sounded a lot like the giant water bug.

"That's gruesome," Eileen said when he finished. "Besides, it's all boys. There won't be any parts for girls."

Mr. Hollis sighed. "All right. That story shows a lot of imagination, Tony. It can be an alternate, if nobody comes up with a problem for the prince. Heather? How about you?"

Tony hunched over his papers. "These idiots wouldn't know a good play if they saw one," he whispered. "I bet I could sell *The Prince of the Ocean and the Bloodsucking Water Warriors* to the movies if I wanted to."

Heather slid down in her seat. "I didn't have any ideas. I liked Eileen's story about the princess."

The Pain gave Tony and me one of her know-it-all looks. She was going to win by default. Even if we all voted for Tony's story, how could we put on a play under water?

I could hear some shouting from the soccer field. Then the chant started. "*Al*-lie, *Al*-lie, *Al*-lie!" I didn't have to look to know what was going on.

"Jeremy," Mr. Hollis said. "How about you?"

"I didn't have a chance to write anything," I said.

Mr. Hollis looked disappointed. "That's too bad. I was counting on your creativity. Didn't you give the play any thought at all?"

There was another burst of cheers from Allie's soccer field, and an idea began to form in my mind. "How about this?" I said. "There's this prince and he's sort of . . . peaceful. He doesn't like wars or even jousting and sword fighting. He lives in a castle with just his father, the king."

"No queen?" Eileen asked.

"The queen died."

Eileen stood up, her hands on her hips. "See, Mr. Hollis? Jeremy's doing it too. They don't want to have any parts for girls. I even have a rhinestone tiara and a long pink satin gown from when I won the Miss Pre-teen Deb contest. It would work for either a princess or a queen. But does Jeremy have any parts for girls? No!"

"There are lots of servants in the castle," I continued. "Some of them could be girls. Besides, the king marries a queen from another kingdom."

Eileen sat down and eyed me suspiciously.

"This queen brings her daughter with her," I said. "She's the same age as the prince."

Eileen brightened up. "This is getting much better, Jeremy. What is the princess like?"

"All she wants to do all day is joust and fight with her sword."

"But that's stupid," Eileen whined. "I couldn't joust and sword-fight in my beautiful long gown."

"Maybe she dresses like a man," Tony said. "Like Maid Marian in *Robin Hood*."

"Yeah, she does," I said, "and the king thinks she's terrific. He always wanted his son to be like that. So the king spends all his time with the new princess and forgets about his real son."

Bruno had arrived in the middle of my story. "I like all that fighting stuff. I could do that." He picked up a stick and pretended to be sword-fighting with a tree.

Mr. Hollis came over and slapped me on the back. "Now that's what I call a good conflict for a story, Jeremy. You have the prince who's been perfectly happy until this princess shows up on the scene and takes all of the king's attention. Now the prince will have to deal with the problem, and that's how you'll develop the plot."

"I know! I know!" Bruno came running back to the table, still brandishing his sword. "There's this dragon who lives outside of town and he's killed a lot of the knights from the kingdom. This princess thinks she's such a hotshot, she goes off to slay the dragon, but instead the dragon kills her. Bingo! End of problem."

"That doesn't work," Heather said. "It's supposed to be a story about the prince, not the princess."

Eileen stuck an elbow in Heather's ribs. "But it could be a very dramatic scene. Maybe the princess could stun the dragon with her beauty and save the kingdom."

"No, Heather's right," I said. "The play is about the prince, and he has to figure out how to handle his stepfamily."

Tony leaned toward me. "I'll say," he whispered out of the side of his mouth. "Especially when the prince's family comes to the play, and they find out they're in it!"

Chapter Nine

That night we all stopped at Abbott's for frozen custard after the game. That was supposed to be a reward for Allie. Half the team was lined up at the windows with their parents. I got a pistachio cone and took Timmy over to sit on a bench where we could watch the people on the miniature golf course.

Allie and Dad were reading a sign that was taped on the window behind me. "It's something I've always wanted to do," Allie said. "You have to let me, Dad."

It made me mad every time I heard Allie call him that. She already had a father. She didn't need mine.

Dad took out a pen and wrote something down. "It sounds good to me, Allie. We'll give these people a call and get the details."

They came over to the bench. "Thanks, Dad," Allie said. "I know I can do it."

"Do what?" I asked.

"Allie wants to enter a kids' triathlon in Casey Park on the Fourth of July."

"What's a triathlon?" Timmy asked.

I was glad he asked, because I didn't know either.

"You start out by swimming an eighth of a mile," Allie said. "Then you jump on a bike and ride on a course outside the park for eight miles. And then at the end, you run two miles on the trails in the park."

"I could do that," Timmy said. "I can do anything, can't I, Kay?"

Kay laughed and wiped the chocolate custard that had melted down Timmy's chin. "This is awfully short notice, Allie. You only have two weeks to train."

"I'm in good shape from soccer, Mom. Besides, living in the country means I've been riding my bike a lot more. I don't know what I'll do about the swimming." She looked at me, as if she expected me to invite her to swim at Tony's. I didn't.

"Are you going to do the tri . . . tri . . . biking, running, swimming thing, Jeremy?" Timmy asked.

"No chance," I said.

Timmy tugged at my hand. "You could do it, Jer. You ride your bike and swim a lot."

"Yeah, but the difference is I do those things for fun. I don't have to prove a point every time I do something." I didn't look up, but I could feel Allie's eyes on me.

"You have to be really competitive to enter an

event like this," Dad said. "That's not Jeremy's thing." He put an arm around Allie. "Come on, Al. I've seen a few of these triathlons on TV. The really big one is in Hawaii every year. I think I have the strategy figured out." The two of them walked off together.

"How's your play coming?" Kay asked, changing the subject.

"Not bad," I said. "They liked my story idea. They're going to use it for the play."

"That's wonderful. Wait until your father hears about this."

"Yeah. I'm sure he'll be thrilled," I said.

Kay smiled and nodded, missing my sarcasm. "What's it about?"

I really didn't want to tell her. Kay would be smart enough to see what I was doing—using our family as a pattern. "Well, it's about this prince," I said, "and he . . ." Luckily I didn't have to go any further, because Dad and Allie came charging back.

"We've got to get home and write out a training schedule," Dad said. He turned to Allie. "This is going to be fun, Al."

Great, I thought. Yet another chance to cheer for Allie's athletic abilities.

The next afternoon, Dad and Allie had their heads together over the kitchen table. Then they went off somewhere in the car. Before long they were back, unloading something in the driveway.

"Where were you?" I asked.

Dad opened the tailgate. "We drove to Webster."

"I needed to go to the bookstore there," I said. "You could have asked me to go along."

"We had to take off in a hurry," Dad said. "We needed time to look around before the store closed."

"What store?" I asked, but I didn't need to wait for an answer. Dad pulled a shiny gold ten-speed racing bike out of the car.

Allie grabbed the handlebars and got on. "I want to try it out, okay, Dad?"

"Hold it, Al," Dad said, ripping open a carton. "Here." He handed her a bike helmet. It was the same gold as the bike.

Allie fastened the chin strap and took off.

"Just take a short ride," Dad called to her. "It'll be getting dark soon."

"How come Allie gets a new bike and I've had the same bike for the last five years?" I asked.

"Yours is still fine for the kind of use you give it," Dad said, watching Allie as she charged down the road.

"I ride my bike every day of my life," I said. "That's how I get around, for pete's sake."

"Yes," Dad said, "but for racing you need a lighter bike, one that's stripped down for speed."

"For this one race, Allie has to have a brand-new hotshot racing bike? And what's wrong with Mom's helmet? It's just like the one I have."

"Don't get so bent out of shape, Jeremy. If Allie's going to be racing, she needs to have the best possible protection." Dad watched Allie as she went over a rise in the road and disappeared. "She's serious about this. This is just the first of many races for Allie. She's a real competitor."

So it didn't matter if I got hit by a truck on my way over to Tony's. As far as Dad was concerned, my old helmet was good enough to hold my head together. It wasn't fair, but I couldn't make myself say anything more to Dad. He had to know how upset I was. He just didn't care.

The gravel stung my legs as Allie pulled back into the driveway, skidding to a stop. "This bike is perfect, Dad. I can't believe how much easier it handles than my old bike. Want to try it, Jeremy?"

Her old bike! It wasn't hers in the first place. "No thanks," I said. I left the two of them to admire Allie's new golden treasure and walked across the back field toward the woods. The last bit of red was fading in the sky, but my eyes adjusted to the dim light.

Dad had said Allie was a real competitor. He was right. She had competed with me for my father's attention and won. It didn't matter that I had a good imagination and I could think up stories to write. That sort of thing wasn't important to Dad. It was important to me, though. I had to make our play so good that even Dad would take notice.

I sat for a long time on the little footbridge over the creek, watching the last birds flying back to their nests for the night. The lights went on in our kitchen and living room. I waited for somebody to notice that I wasn't home and call out the back door for me. Nobody did. I could hear tractor trailers up on the main highway and a couple of cats fighting in the distance. Sounds carried a long way in the country, especially at night. Pretty soon the moon came up. It was almost full.

I got up and started toward the house, but I realized there was enough moonlight filtering through the branches to show the way into the woods. I turned around and headed toward Mom's special place. As I walked down the path, I pictured myself going back through the centuries. By the time I reached the clearing, my imagination had taken over. I was Prince Andrew.

I knew how he felt the day the new queen came with her daughter. I even gave the prince a little brother who was just as taken in by the queen as Timmy was with Kay. I climbed up onto a low maple-tree branch and pretended it was a tower where I could watch the queen's daughter practice jousting down below. She won every match, knocking the king's knights off their horses one by one.

Weeks went by, and the king acted colder and colder to me. I tried to tell him about the things that interested me, but he didn't care. He only had time for his new stepdaughter.

My little brother wanted to spend all his time with

the queen. Then the queen started changing everything around in the castle, so all traces of my mother were erased. Now it looked like the kingdom that the queen had come from—foreign and strange.

Finally the kingdom's summer festival began. The highlight of the day was the jousting tournament with all the knights of the kingdom. The king gave the fastest and strongest horse in the kingdom to the princess, and outfitted both her and her horse in armor made of gold. He gave me nothing.

I climbed slowly up to the tower, my ears ringing with the clash of armor as the queen's daughter knocked the knights from their horses onto the hard dirt.

The king was so busy cheering, he didn't even wonder where I was. He'll be sorry, I thought, as I crept out onto the ledge. The king glanced up at me for a second, then looked away, as if he didn't even recognize me as his son. I took a deep breath and jumped down from my branch. In my mind, I plunged hundreds of feet to the ground right into the middle of the tournament field. I was killed instantly.

The king suddenly realized what he had done. He banished the queen and her daughter from the kingdom.

No, that was no good. If I was killed, I wouldn't be able to enjoy seeing the queen and her daughter plead with the king for forgiveness. I replayed the scene in my head. This time I wasn't killed, but every bone in my body was broken.

No, that would be too painful. Maybe I just broke a few minor bones, but it was enough to jolt the king into realizing what he had done. That was it!

The king came rushing down from the grand-stand. "My son, thank heaven you're still alive," he cried. "This is all my fault."

I managed to smile weakly.

He turned to the queen and her daughter. "If you hadn't come here, this never would have happened. I have the most wonderful son in the world, and I've been ignoring him. I wish I'd never laid eyes on either of you. Get out of my kingdom."

The king grabbed the reins of a horse from one of his fallen knights. He swung the queen up into the saddle, and pushed her daughter up behind her. Then he smacked the horse on the rear. "Get out of my sight before I kill you both."

I just lay there on the ground for a few minutes, breathing hard from the emotion of the scene. Then as soon as I caught my breath, I ran back to my room and put it down on paper—every word, just the way I'd imagined it. It was great!

I could hardly wait to read my play to the rest of the kids on Thursday night. Tony had been bugging me about it all week, but I didn't want him to hear it ahead of time. He kept it up when I went over to help him sort out the day's insect catch Thursday morning.

"You're playing with fire, Jeremy. You know that, don't you?"

"What do you mean?"

Tony studied a neon green bug with his magnifying glass. "The idea you had about the prince and the new queen who comes with her daughter. That's your family you're talking about." He picked up the bug with tweezers. "Maybe the other people in the group don't know you well enough to see it, but I do. What if your dad and Kay find out about it?"

"They won't go to the play," I said. "Allie will be on the seventh-grade soccer team this fall. Her games should keep them busy enough to ignore me."

Tony put down the magnifying glass. "You're not being fair, Jeremy. Your father has always done lots of stuff with us, like taking us fishing and going on hikes at the Cummings Nature Center."

"Yeah, but that's all over, Tony. You don't see him doing anything with us now, do you?"

"He's probably just trying to be nice to Allie until she feels at home here."

"He's making her feel at home, all right." I told Tony about the triathlon and the new bike Dad got Allie to ride in it.

"Maybe you're right," Tony said. "It sounds as if Allie's taking over. But it's partly your fault, because you're just letting it happen. You have to get your dad's attention."

"Sure, but how?"

"I don't know," Tony said. "I'll think of something."

When we arrived at the meeting that night, I volunteered to read first. I made a real production out of it. I even used different voices for the characters, the way I did for Timmy's stories. When I finished, I thought everybody would clap, but they didn't.

"You put a lot of work into this, Jeremy," Mr. Hollis said. He looked around the group. "So, what do the rest of you think?"

"I think it's stupid," Tony said.

"Some best friend you are," I muttered.

Mr. Hollis leaned forward with his elbows on his knees. "You want to elaborate on that remark, Tony?"

"I don't like the way it ends. What's the use? Prince Andrew didn't prove anything. He just jumped out of a tower and hurt himself to get sympathy. What good is that?"

"It makes the king see what he did," I said. "Now the king will feel bad for the rest of his life, and that's just what he deserves."

"But that doesn't prove anything," Tony said.

"Andrew should have talked to his father and told him how he felt."

"He couldn't talk to him," I said. "The king was too busy with his new daughter to listen. He finally had the kind of kid he always wanted."

Tony sat back in his seat and glared at me. "I still say it's a stupid ending."

Eileen started gathering up her things. "Well, that's it. I quit. Who ever heard of a princess who likes jousting? Come on, Heather. Let's go."

"I like it," Heather said quietly, then ducked her head, avoiding Eileen's glare.

"Go on, Heather," Mr. Hollis said. "Let's hear what you think."

Heather looked up. "Well, I like the idea, because it could happen today. There are so many kids whose parents are divorced and remarried. And it's hard . . ." She looked down at her folded hands on the table. "It's hard having stepbrothers and stepsisters, even if they don't live with you all the time. I have to go to my father's house every other weekend, and his new wife has a couple of kids who hate my guts. I hate theirs, too." She ducked her head again. "But I don't like the ending either."

"How do you think it should end?" Mr. Hollis asked.

Heather thought for a minute. "The prince needs to prove he's worth as much or more than the queen's daughter, and he doesn't do that by jumping off a tower. Maybe if he doesn't like jousting, he could do something else to show he's brave."

"That's a good idea," Tony said. "He could go on a quest."

"Yes!" Eileen's eyes lit up. "He could rescue a beautiful princess from a dragon. I mean the kind of princess who wears a gorgeous long gown and a diamond tiara."

"Forget the princess," Heather said. "You only want a princess so you can play the part."

"She could be the dragon," Bruno said, and everybody laughed.

Eileen slid to the end of the bench and sulked. "My mother and I aren't bringing you anymore, Heather."

"Fine. I'll ride my bike," Heather said, moving over to our table. "The quest is a great idea, because the prince could prove to his father that he has courage."

"But I liked it the way it was," I said. "I want the queen and her daughter to be banished from the kingdom."

Mr. Hollis smiled. "Now we're getting somewhere. Jeremy, I know you're upset that people don't like your ending, but this is what writing is all about. To make a good story, you have to keep revising it and changing it until it's the best it can possibly be. Even if you were writing about something from real life, you should use your imagination to change it and make something new. Do you understand the points the other people have been making?"

"I guess," I said. For a second I thought Mr. Hollis knew about Allie, but then I realized he was just talking about writing in general.

"All right," Mr. Hollis said. "What should the quest be?"

Heather raised her hand. "Well, whatever it is, it should have three parts. In the books I've read, the quest almost always has three parts."

Mr. Hollis nodded. "Good observation, Heather. In the classic stories, there are usually three things that the hero has to do in order to reach his goal."

We tossed around ideas for the quest for a while, but the other kids' rides came before we could decide on anything. Tony and I hung around until the others had left. Tony said he needed to talk to me, and he didn't want to do it at home.

"Listen," he said, waving as Mr. Hollis pulled out of the parking lot. "I've got it."

"Got what?"

"I've figured out how you're going to win back your father. You need a quest. And I know just what it's going to be."

"You're talking crazy, Tony."

"No, I'm not. You need a quest with three parts to it. Does that ring any bells?"

"No."

"This is so perfect, Jeremy. You're going to enter the triathlon."

"Why would I do that? So Allie could humiliate me in front of more people than ever?" I started to get my bike, but Tony stopped me.

"Think about it, Jer. She can beat you on the playing field, because she's much better than you in soccer. But you can do all the events in a triathlon. You've been riding bikes, swimming and running all your life."

"You're nuts, Tony. Competing with Allie in anything athletic would be suicide."

All the way home, Tony tried to convince me. "I'll even help you train, Jer. We'll ride bikes every day and I'll borrow my brother's stopwatch so I can check your time. You can practice laps in our pool, and we can go up to the high school track to run."

I held my ground. Nothing that Tony said could convince me. Then that night I had a dream. I entered the triathlon with Allie. First, I left her behind in the swim. I was starting off on the bike course before she even got out of the water. I wasn't even out of breath when I finished the bike lap and began running. I felt as if my feet had wings. I passed all the other runners and broke through the ribbon at the finish line. Dad ran over to me. I finally saw on his face what I'd been looking for all along. He was proud of me!

Chapter Ten

Flashes of the dream kept coming back to me all morning. It seemed crazy, but I began to believe I could beat Allie in the triathlon. After all, as Tony said, I already knew how to run, ride and swim. How hard could it be?

After lunch, I went to tell Tony I had decided to compete, but I kept the dream a secret. "All right!" He jumped up from the bug table on the porch, almost spilling the day's new catch. "I knew you'd come to your senses if you thought about it. Look what I made last night." He pulled a folded piece of paper out of his pocket.

"If this is more of your bloodsucking water warriors . . ."

"This is your training map, Jer. I worked it all out from a map of the town. First we start out with a two-mile course. That's about the distance between our houses, so you're used to it. Then we add a mile to the course each day until we get up to eight. By the time you get to the real race, it'll be a piece of cake."

Tony had the two-week training program all planned out. For a nonathlete, he made a pretty good coach. He had me swim back and forth across his pool every day until I could do twenty-seven laps without stopping. That equaled the eighth of a mile I would have to do in the race.

It practically killed me at first, but by the end of the first week I was getting stronger. Tony timed me from the deck with a stopwatch. "You just shaved seven seconds off your time from yesterday. If you keep up this pace, you'll win for sure."

I hauled myself onto the deck, and stretched out to catch my breath. "I don't expect to win this thing, Tony. I just want to beat Allie. You'll have to let me know if she's gaining on me in the race, because I won't be able to turn around and look for her."

Tony polished the face of the watch on his shirt. "I've . . . um . . . been meaning to tell you about that. I won't be at the race, because our family is going away for the Fourth of July."

I sat up, stunned. "You're kidding! You got me into this in the first place. I need you there for moral support."

"You're not going to be alone, Jer. Your whole family will be there."

"Have you noticed how much moral support I've been getting from my family lately? Zip!"

Tony grabbed his bug-fishing net and slipped into

the pool. "Maybe you should start training with your dad and Allie, anyway."

"Why would I want to do that? I like training with you."

"That's the other thing I wanted to tell you," Tony said, moving across the pool with his back to me. "My dad got three extra vacation days for the overtime he's been working."

"So?"

Tony turned to face me. "So we're leaving tomorrow. I'm sorry, Jer."

I was so discouraged the next day, I didn't even practice biking or running. Swimming was out, because I wasn't allowed to use the Cibulas' pool when the family wasn't home. Dad was spending every spare minute training with Allie. She never even asked to use Tony's pool, so I figured they were going someplace else for swimming.

The next couple of days I ran and biked, but it wasn't the same without Tony keeping track of my times. Maybe Tony was right about me training with Dad and Allie. Allie was doing stretches on the front steps Saturday morning. "Where are you going to run?" I asked.

"Down the road to the Weber farm and then back," Allie said. "That makes exactly two miles."

Dad looked up from tying his sneakers. "Jeremy,

I haven't had a chance to work in the garden all week. Will you pick beans while we're gone? The plants will stop producing if we just let them go."

"But Dad, I was just going to ask if I could go running with you and Allie."

Dad slapped me on the back. "That's a good one. Anything to get out of working in the garden, huh?"

Allie laughed and shook her head.

"Don't make fun of me," I said. "I wasn't kidding."

"I'm sorry, Jeremy," Dad said. "I didn't realize you were serious. Ordinarily I'd love to have you come along, but Allie's worked up to a pretty fast pace by now. We only have two days until the big race. After it's over I'll work out with you. But right now, I really need to have you pick those beans. Kay wants to freeze them today."

He started his stopwatch, and the two of them took off down the road.

I grabbed a basket and headed for the garden. All of a sudden I was being treated like Cinderella. "Stay home and do the chores while your wicked stepsister goes to the ball." I'd show them both on Monday. I couldn't wait to see Dad's face when he found out I was entering the triathlon.

Monday morning dawned with the drumming of rain on the roof. It cleared a little by afternoon, but there was still a chill in the air. I put on my bathing trunks with shorts over them.

Dad was fastening Allie's bike on the rack when I pulled mine out of the garage. "Don't take that along today, Jeremy. It's going to be too confusing with all the people in the race."

"I'm going to be in the race," I said.

"Don't kid around, Jeremy. Give me a hand with this bike rack, will you? One of the bolts is loose."

"I'm not kidding, Dad. I'm entering the triathlon." I waited to see the look of pride break across his face, but it didn't happen.

"You just can't decide to enter an event like this at the last second," Dad said. "Allie's been training for two weeks."

"Maybe I've been training, too," I said.

Dad sighed. "This is just like you, Jeremy. Why didn't you say something earlier? You don't have the proper equipment. I could have at least checked out your chain and gears." Dad looked at his watch. "It's too late. If we don't leave right now, we'll miss the registration." He clamped my bike on the rack next to Allie's, and we climbed into the car.

What did Dad mean by "proper equipment"? Was he trying to pretend he would have bought a fancy new bike for me, too, if he'd known I was racing? Fat chance!

Dad spent the whole drive over to the park giving Allie advice about how to handle the race in the rain.

Every now and then he'd add, "You too, Jeremy," as an afterthought.

"Why are you doing this, anyway?" Allie asked, as we waited in line to register.

"Because I want to. I can ride a bike, I can run and I can swim. I have just as much right to be in this thing as you."

Allie shrugged. "Who said you didn't?"

There were a lot more kids entering the triathlon than I'd expected. Allie and I were competing against eleven- through fourteen-year-olds. Some of the guys in line looked pretty big.

The sky was cloudy, and it wasn't actually raining, but the air was filled with a cold mist—the kind that soaks right through your clothes. After registering, Allie and I put our bikes in the rack, where we'd pick them up after the swim.

I could tell Allie was nervous. She was constantly moving—stretching, shaking her arms and legs or jogging in place.

A voice on a loudspeaker called everybody over to the starting area on the side of the pond for final instructions. We were divided into groups according to our ages. The older kids were first. There were about twenty people in each group, or "wave," as they called it. Each wave had to line up in a chute marked off with yellow plastic tape on fence posts. It reminded me of the picture of cattle stockyards in our social studies book.

Allie and I were in wave number four. "I don't get it," I said. "If the big kids get to start first, how could we possibly catch up?"

"We don't catch up," Allie said. "They keep track of our total time, and the fastest one wins. They just let the older kids go first so they don't plow through the younger ones in the swim. A quarter mile is a long swim for little kids."

"Did you say a quarter mile?"

Allie nodded.

"I thought this was supposed to be an eighth of a mile."

"I did too, at first. I read it wrong on the poster."

"Did you practice swimming that far?" I asked.

"Sure. I came over here every day. They've had the course marked off all week. Didn't you see it? You go around those yellow markers."

A line of yellow floats led partway across the pond, then made a right angle to the beach. Pairs of lifeguards were stationed in rowboats all along the course, and a couple of them were standing on a float near the finish. I noticed that the town ambulance was waiting up by the bike area.

The official gave a two-minute call, and the first group of kids plunged in, then got out and stood ready with their toes touching the edge of the water. When the starting gun went off, all I could see was the splashing of arms and legs. It didn't take long to see who the good swimmers were. Two or three of them sliced through the water like sharks, way out ahead of the others.

The gun went off again, and the second wave of kids took off. I could feel my heart starting to pound. The muscles in the back of Allie's neck stood out like bungee cords. I felt just the opposite, as if every muscle in my body had gone limp. I could barely stand up.

The third shot went off. "Come on," Allie said. "Our wave will be next. We just have time to get used to the water." She plunged in and swam out a few yards. So did everybody else in our wave, except me.

I waded in. The water turned my feet numb. I splashed water over my shoulders and chest. It was so cold, I wouldn't have been surprised to see ice cubes floating on the surface. Suddenly my muscles woke up and started shaking. I got out of the water and stood there with my arms wrapped around myself. I was shivering so hard, I must have looked like I was having a seizure.

I took a deep breath and charged right in when our starting gun went off. Within the first minute, I was kicked in the face seven times. Gradually the splashing calmed down as all the other kids in my wave left me behind. I kept forging ahead, pretending I was going across Tony's pool. Then the wake from the other swimmers sloshed over my head and I began coughing. I automatically tried to put my feet down, but the bottom had dropped away, and I went under. I choked and sputtered to the surface, frantically thrashing in the water. Within seconds, one of the lifeguard rowboats came up next to me. A tanned, blond kid leaned out. "You okay?"

I nodded my head, still coughing.

"I won't pull you out if you don't want to quit," he said, "because that would disqualify you from the rest of the race. Just tread water for a few minutes. It'll help you catch your breath."

When the coughing finally died down, I tried to swim again. I couldn't see the rest of the kids in my wave. There wasn't even a ripple in the water ahead of me. I could hear people cheering from the beach. Allie was probably out of the water and on her bike by now.

Suddenly the gun went off. Before I knew what was happening, I was surrounded by a whole new group of swimmers. I moved out of their way so I wouldn't get kicked. I lost time doing that, and now I was off course.

"This way," a lifeguard said. It was a different boat now—a girl this time. "Go to your left," she said.

I did as I was told and kept going. All I cared about was finishing.

"Go, Jeremy, go!" It was Timmy's voice. I could just barely make him out standing on the beach with Kay and Dad.

"Come on, Jeremy," Dad yelled. "You can do it."

There was another lifeguard boat next to me now. The guards were passing me along like a baton in a relay race. A tall black kid leaned out over the bow. "I'm Scott, Jeremy. How are you doing? You want to keep going or call it quits?"

"Keep going," I gasped.

He gave me a thumbs-up sign. "That's my man."

I heard the gun go off again. This time it took a little longer for the swimmers to reach me. The water got choppy, and I swallowed some again.

I felt as if my insides had been sucked out by a giant water bug. I was just a piece of skin in a bathing suit, bobbing around on the rough surface.

Scott's boat slid silently next to me again. "Swim on your back for a while, Jeremy. That way you can save your strength for a strong finish." I rolled over onto my back and felt the water gurgling in my ears.

The sound of the gun rang in my ears, and Scott turned to watch the next group approach. "You're out of my territory now, Jeremy. The guards on the float will help you. It's not much farther to the end."

I was exhausted. Now I understood how a person could drown. You probably got so tired you just gave up and went to sleep. I felt my eyes closing.

Then a voice from somewhere inside my head said, "Remember your quest!" Suddenly I was Prince Andrew. At the other shore, a wild horse stamped his hooves and whinnied, waiting to take me on the next leg of my journey. In the distance I could see the castle where I'd lived with my father. I had to prove myself if I wanted to go back and live in that castle again.

My arms picked up a rhythm and I finally felt like I was swimming rather than drowning. I swam with my eyes closed. The last lifeguards kept shouting directions to keep me on course. Every now and then I could hear Timmy's voice or Dad's or Kay's, urging me on. They must have stayed with me rather than going to watch Allie on the bike. Allie would be mad about that. She liked an audience.

Everyone on the beach was rooting for me now. "Come on, Jeremy," they called.

"Almost there!"

"Keep it up."

I finally had a crowd cheering for me, but it didn't have the same excitement as the crowd that cheered for Allie's runs down the soccer field.

Suddenly my foot hit the bottom of the pond. It was over. I dragged myself out of the water and staggered up the beach. "You did it!" Timmy shouted. "I thought you were going to drown, Jeremy." He was running along next to me with Kay and Dad just behind.

"Don't try to do the rest of the course, Jeremy," Kay said. "You're exhausted."

"Let him go, Kay," Dad said. "The hard part is over, Jeremy. Don't give up. You can make it."

I stumbled into the parking lot. There were only

a few bikes left. For all I knew, some of their owners could be doing the running lap already. Just as I reached my bike, a couple of riders came in, jammed their bikes into the rack and started off on the running trail that circled inside the park. I stuffed my feet into my sneakers, put on my helmet and took off on my bike.

My legs pumped like a machine. I didn't even feel them. I gradually calmed my breathing down as I rode. Sometime during my swim, the rain had stopped. The sun was out in full force now, making the air steamy. I followed the bike course markers out of the park. There were arrows painted on the road to show us where to go.

When I turned the next corner, a bunch of people were waiting with paper cups of water. A guy ran out to hand me one, but I was so wobbly, I couldn't let go of the handlebar to grab it.

I took a deep breath. I was Prince Andrew again, and I was riding my horse through a tropical forest where wild animals crouched ready to spring at me. My horse and I kept going, fearless. "Come on, boy," I said. "We have to make it. We just have to."

I put on a burst of speed and got a cramp in my side. I slowed down, but it didn't go away. My legs wouldn't work right anymore. I stopped and sat under a big shade tree, doubling over in pain.

"Jeremy? You all right?" It was Allie.

"What are you doing here?" I asked.

"When I finished the race, I saw that your bike

wasn't on the rack, so I grabbed mine and came looking for you. Mom and Dad were worried."

I wasn't even halfway through the bike course and Allie had finished the whole stupid race. What ever made me think I could beat her at anything? I couldn't stand it anymore. I couldn't stand *her*. "Stop calling him 'Dad,' " I said. "How many fathers do you need? You already have your own father."

Allie stared at me, her mouth half open.

I propped myself up on my elbows. "I mean it. Who the heck do you think you are? The big super athlete comes and takes over my father. Why don't you go live with your own dad?"

Allie stood there, straddling her bike. "Maybe I will someday, not that it's any of your business."

"Why wait?" I asked. "Why not go right now?"

"Look," Allie said, her eyes narrowing. "I told you before, I don't want to talk about my father."

"You don't know where he is, do you?" I said. "I bet he ran off and left you and Kay and you haven't seen him since."

"Of course I know where he is." Allie gripped her handlebars so tightly her knuckles turned white. "He just has a new family, that's all. They have four kids. They're too far away to visit now."

For a second, I thought she was going to cry. Then she yanked on the chin strap of her helmet to tighten it. "I'll go tell Mom and . . . your father that you're okay."

She started to ride off, then circled around and came back. "You know something? The whole time I was growing up, I had to come home to an empty house every day after school. When I found out I was going to have brothers, I was so happy. I'd never have to be in an empty house again. I didn't know I'd be getting a brother who hated me." Allie's eyes cut right through me. "You don't deserve your father, Jeremy. He's wonderful, and you don't even care." She turned and rode away, her head down as if she were sprinting for an imaginary finish line.

What was that supposed to mean? I didn't deserve my father? Well, fine. She could have him. She could have the whole family. Nobody wanted me, anyway.

When I stood up, my legs still felt funny, but the pain in my side was gone. I grabbed my bike and started off, but somehow finishing the race didn't seem important. Coming in last wasn't going to impress anybody and the quest idea had been dumb in the first place. I didn't feel like the prince anymore. I felt like what I was—a loser.

I followed the course slowly back to the park, coasting every time there was a dip in the road. I hadn't dried my feet off after the swim, and there was sand inside my sneakers. I could feel it rubbing the skin off my heels. I pulled up to a small creek and dipped my feet in the cool water. I sat there for a while, launching leaf boats downstream.

Finally I headed back for the park. As I got closer,

I heard a loudspeaker. The prizes were about to be awarded. I couldn't stand to see Allie get a trophy.

I spotted Kay, Timmy and Dad having a big discussion with Allie. She was probably giving them a blow-by-blow description of her race. They wouldn't miss me. When you have a superstar daughter, you don't need a loser son.

Chapter Eleven

A small dirt road off the parking lot led back to the place where Dad used to take Tony and me fishing. I decided to take it rather than face my family. I could still hear the loudspeaker as I rode into the woods, but the trees muffled the words, so I wouldn't have to hear Allie's name announced. I kept going until the road turned into a path and came out on the bank of the pond. I left my bike and climbed out onto our old fishing rock.

I didn't know what to do anymore. Maybe I was old enough to go off on my own. I'd read lots of books about kids who had done that. Back in King Arthur's time, I'd be considered almost a man at my age. Maybe I should sneak home while nobody was there, pack up some clothes and take off. But take off to where? I'd seen programs on TV about runaways who went to big cities and got into all kinds of trouble. And where would I live?

The barbecue was starting now, and the smell of

barbecued chicken came all the way back to me in the woods. I hadn't realized how hungry I was. I'd be hungry all the time if I ran away.

Maybe Tony's family would let me move in with them. Except they had so many kids already, I'd have to sleep on the floor of Tony and his brothers' room. There wasn't even space for another bed. They hardly ever cleaned their room, so I'd be breathing dust bunnies all night.

I sat for a long time tossing rocks into the water, listening to their deep "thunk." The sun was skimming the trees on the opposite bank, turning the sky red. A damp chill was coming back into the air. Dad said the best times to fish were early in the morning and just before the sun went down. Since he always went to work in the morning, he used to take Tony and me fishing at the end of the day.

I could picture the three of us sitting on the flat rock, whispering so we wouldn't scare off the fish. Fat chance of that happening again, now that all of Dad's spare time was taken up with Allie.

I could hear bits of laughter and talk from the main part of the park, and the smell of chicken was really getting to me. I walked my bike along the bank and climbed up to see what was going on. It looked as if the whole town was in Casey Park. People who hadn't been there for the race had come for the barbecue and for the fireworks that were going to start as soon as it got dark.

Somebody must have been selling green bracelets

that glowed in the dark. A lot of kids were running around wearing them and tossing them up in the air. It looked like a scene from outer space. Here and there I could see the bright fizz of sparklers, and firecrackers popped in the distance.

I didn't go over to where the people were. I just couldn't face my family right now, and they obviously didn't care about me. Nobody had even tried to find me, and I'd been gone almost two hours. If Dad knew me at all, he would have known that I'd gone to our old fishing spot. That just showed it never had meant as much to him as it did to me.

Suddenly I saw a figure running toward me. I slid down the bank, but he followed, kicking loose a shower of small stones. It was Dad. "Jeremy! I thought that was you. Kay and I have been frantic looking for you."

"Yeah, right," I mumbled.

Dad slid down the rest of the bank, catching his balance at the bottom. "Kay and I were so concerned about you in the swim. I almost followed you on the bike ride, but you're so independent, I didn't think you'd want me coming after you. Allie said you were all right when she saw you. But when you didn't come back for so long, I went out looking. I drove all over the course. I even looked for you at home and checked at Tony's house. Where the heck were you?"

"I stopped to rest for a few minutes," I said, not looking up. "That's probably when you drove by."

"Jeremy, I was around that course at least four times. You've been hiding out. Why?"

I turned my back to him. "Maybe I didn't want to watch Allie add to her trophy collection. What did she do, come in first?"

"No, as a matter of fact, she came in ninth. The trophies were only for the first three finishers."

"That must have been disappointing for you after getting the new bike and spending all that time training her," I said sarcastically.

"Is that what this is all about, Jeremy? You're upset because I bought Allie a bike?"

"I don't care about the bike, Dad—it's the time." I turned to face him. "You spend every spare minute with Allie."

"There's a reason I've spent so much time with her, Jeremy. I've been trying to make up for all those years she didn't have a father."

"Yeah, I know," I said. "Poor little orphan Allie."

"You're not being fair to Allie. This isn't like you."

The anger I'd been pushing down for so long came boiling over. "I've had it, all right? I can't compete with Allie, because I'm lousy in sports. You love everything she does. You're trying to make her into the son you always wanted. Did you realize you're even calling her 'Al'?"

"Don't be silly, Jeremy. That's just a nickname. Besides, I've been giving extra attention to Allie because I'm trying to make her feel at home. She's not used to having a father around."

"Neither am I!" I shouted. "You haven't been a father since Mom died."

Dad looked as if he'd been punched in the stomach. "How can you say that? I've tried to keep everything the same for you and Timmy."

"Keep it the same? To make it seem like Mom's getting killed wasn't a big deal?"

"No, that's not it at all. Of course it was a big deal. We were all devastated. I just tried to keep things on an even keel."

"A boat can still sink with an even keel, Dad. It can just spring a leak and drop to the bottom like a stone. That's what happened to our family. I'm talking about our real family. Just you and me and Timmy."

"Don't be so dramatic, Jeremy. We've come through all right."

"Oh, yeah. We're just great. Timmy doesn't even remember Mom. Did you know that? He thinks Kay is his mother. And you! You're fine now, aren't you? You got somebody to take Mom's place, so what do you care?"

For the first time in my life, my father raised his hand and slapped me hard across my face. I tried to scramble back up the bank, but he caught my arm. I thought he was going to hit me again, but instead, he ran his hand gently over my cheek where the slap still stung. "You think I don't care, Jeremy? There isn't a day that goes by that I don't think of your mother."

"You didn't even cry," I said, choking down a sob. "Right after the funeral, when all the relatives came back to the house, it was like a party. Everybody brought food and told funny stories about things Mom did. They were laughing and stuffing their faces as if nothing had happened. You were the worst one of all, Dad. Grandma kept crying and you'd remind her of something funny to make her laugh. I never saw you cry once."

"Jeremy, I thought you knew—that's what people do when somebody they love dies. We were just trying to share our memories of your mother to keep her alive inside of us."

"They why didn't you ever do that with Timmy and me? You never talk about her, Dad. You let her memory die. Now we don't have anything left of her."

"I don't talk about her because . . ." Dad closed his eyes. "I should have, but I couldn't. If I didn't let myself think about her, I didn't have to feel the pain. I wanted to pretend she was just away for a while."

He reached out to me, and I put my arms around him. I noticed that my arms had grown since the last time I had hugged him, so that my fingers touched behind his back. "I do the same thing, Dad. Sometimes I think I hear her car coming in the driveway." I buried my face in his Buffalo Bills sweatshirt and could feel him sobbing with me.

"You're the one who held us together when your

mother died," Dad said, after a few minutes had passed.

"Me?"

"You were so good with Timmy, reading to him and playing with him. You reached him in ways that I couldn't. I should have realized what you were going through, but you didn't show it."

I pulled back and wiped my eyes with the back of my hand. "I used to cry alone in my room with my door closed. I didn't want you to know that I was upset."

Dad nodded. "I used to do the same thing. Maybe we should have cried together."

We stood there in silence for a few minutes, then Dad reached over and brushed the hair out of my eyes. "We have to work harder at telling each other what we're thinking from now on, Jeremy. We've opened a door, and now we have to keep it open. I thought you knew how much I loved you. It's just hard for me to talk about it."

"You're not ashamed of me?" I asked.

"How could I be ashamed? You have your own talents, like writing that play. Mr. Hollis said you're the one with all the ideas. That's really something."

There was a sudden flash, followed by a loud boom. In the light from the fireworks, I saw the look of pride on Dad's face.

Another rocket exploded over the water. Where we were standing, we could see its reflection in the pond. As the silver sparkles dropped from the sky, the ones in the reflection went up to meet them. Some of the embers made it all the way to the water before blinking out. I watched it happen over and over again, standing there with Dad, listening to the distant "oooh" from the crowd each time a rocket exploded.

Suddenly I knew how to end the play. The queen and the princess wouldn't be banished this time. Prince Andrew would fail in his quest, and he'd have it out with the king, just like Dad and me. And then maybe they'd understand each other better, and the prince would have his father back. Prince Andrew could try harder to get along with the princess, too. Her life hadn't been any fairy tale, so that might account for the way she acted. Then, as time went by, they'd all learn how to become a family.

As I always told Timmy, you can make anything happen in your imagination. If that was true, maybe I could make it happen in real life.